Dear Reader,

I just wanted to tell you how delighted I am that my
publisher has decided to reprint so many of my earlier
books. Some of them have not been available for a while,
and amongst them there are titles that have often been
requested.

I can't remember a time when I haven't written, although
it was not until my daughter was born that I felt confident
enough to attempt to get anything published. With my
husband's encouragement, my first book was accepted,
and since then there have been over 130 more.

Not that the thrill of having a book published gets
any less. I still feel the same excitement when a new
manuscript is accepted. But it's you, my readers, to
whom I owe so much. Your support—and particularly
your letters—give me so much pleasure.

I hope you enjoy this collection of some of my favorite
novels.

Anne Mather

Back by Popular Demand

With a phenomenal one hundred and thirty-five books published by Harlequin, Anne Mather is one of the world's most popular romance authors. Harlequin is proud to bring back many of these highly sought-after novels in a special Collector's Edition.

Anne MATHER

COLLECTOR'S EDITION

THE SHROUDED WEB

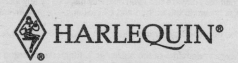

HARLEQUIN®

TORONTO • NEW YORK • LONDON
AMSTERDAM • PARIS • SYDNEY • HAMBURG
STOCKHOLM • ATHENS • TOKYO • MILAN • MADRID
PRAGUE • WARSAW • BUDAPEST • AUCKLAND

ISBN 0-373-63152-9

THE SHROUDED WEB

First North American Publication 1976.

Copyright © 1973 by Anne Mather.

Visit us at www.eHarlequin.com

Printed in U.S.A.

CHAPTER ONE

IT WAS A bare room, scantily furnished and uncarpeted, and yet it had represented a return to normality, to peace; to escape from the horrifying reality of the holocaust he had lived through. During the past few days he had had many opportunities to study this room, but only now, as his body began to make demands upon him again, did he begin to notice its limitations.

The nuns who had cared for him, who had nursed him back to health, had been marvellous. And after all, this was their environment, not his. They chose to live without anything but the bare necessities of life, dedicating themselves to the service of God and their fellow human beings.

But something, some inner knowledge told him that this had not been his way. He had been used to a much different kind of existence, and his head ached with his determination to remember exactly what that existence had been. No amount of kindness, of care and attention, could assuage his depression at the realisation that he could remember nothing before the plane crash, and although the doctor had said that this was not an unusual occurrence and that his memory

5

could return at any time, as the days went by he could feel himself losing confidence in that prognosis.

They had told him about the crash, of course. He had had horrifying nightmares when he was first brought down the mountain to the little mission hospital, and they had had to tell him that there had been no other survivors. He had been delirious, of course, breaking out in a sweat every time he heard the sound of an aircraft overhead, but gradually the horror had receded, and in its place had come an almost guilty feeling of relief, followed by an intense curiosity. The morose depression of the amnesiac was only now embracing him.

In the beginning he had not understood the language spoken by the nuns and the swarthy-skinned doctor, but they had eventually explained to him in stilted English that the plane had crashed while crossing the Andes in South America, and that the hospital was in the mountain district of Monteraverde, a small Portuguese-speaking country situated on the borders of Bolivia and Paraguay. They had not been able to tell him why he should have been on that plane making such a journey, and as all the records had been burnt in the terrible fire which followed the crash, they had no way of knowing his identity. But for all that, they continually exclaimed at the miracle of his survival, and he knew he ought to feel grateful, too.

The authorities had been informed, of course, but

the plane had belonged to a Brazilian company and things moved more slowly here, miles from the bustling metropolis of Rio de Janeiro. There had been other English people on the aircraft, too, which made things more difficult, and until full enquiries could be made he might be one of several people. It was disturbing and frustrating, and as his strength returned his mind and body rebelled at the continued delay. Something told him he was not a patient man, that he was a man more accustomed to giving orders rather than taking them, and he was impatient to discover his identity and get on with his life. Only occasionally he allowed the rather terrifying possibility of his not regaining his memory to envelop him, and then his depression assumed shattering proportions.

The door to his room opened just then to admit one of the nuns. This was Sister Teresa, and she moved smoothly to his bed, eyes averted. It was strange how he could retain the remembrance of everything since the crash with piercing clarity, almost as though because he had no previous recollections to fill his mind, anything that happened now had an increased degree of importance. Sister Teresa was young, no more than twenty-two or three, he estimated, and he knew also that she found it difficult to maintain her air of coolness and composure beneath the appraising glint of his grey eyes. But because she had been to a convent school in the United States and therefore could speak good English, she was invariably left to attend to his needs.

That was strange too, he thought inconsequently. One would have thought that when one lost one's memory, all previous knowledge would of necessity be obliterated. But it was not so. He knew what the United States represented; he understood what was meant by a convent school; it was only his own experiences which had been temporarily erased.

'Good afternoon, *senhor*,' Sister Teresa was saying now. 'And how are you feeling?'

He sighed, moving restlessly against the pillows which supported his head and shoulders. The ache in his head which had been so painfully evident in the early days after the crash, owing to an ugly bruise on his forehead, was gradually losing its paralysing effect, and apart from a general feeling of weakness he felt almost well enough to be up and about.

'I'm much better,' he replied, running a questing hand over the growth of beard on his jawline. So far no one had attempted to shave him and the dark stubble irritated him. 'When am I to be allowed up? Sister Maria who was here this morning didn't seem to understand a word I said!'

Sister Teresa raised her eyes. She had rather nice eyes set in a narrow face that while not being beautiful had a gentle charm about it. 'Sister Maria does not speak English, *senhor*,' she explained carefully. 'But I was assisting Doctor Ramirez with an operation, and was unable to attend to you myself.' She folded her hands within the sleeves of her habit. 'I think perhaps it will be several days yet before the doctor will allow you to get up, *senhor*. You must remember that your body sustained a terrible shock—'

'But I feel perfectly all right.' He controlled his impatience with difficulty. 'Nobody seems to realise the urgency involved. Has it occurred to nobody that there must have been a reason for my visit to South America? That at this moment, someone, somewhere, is possibly anxious about my whereabouts?'

'We understand this, of course, *senhor*.' Sister Teresa was infuriatingly calm. 'It is understandable that you should want to recover your memory and resume your usual activities. But has it also occurred to you that were someone particularly anxious to learn of your whereabouts they would have made enquiries?'

'But how much publicity will the crash have been given in the European press?' he demanded scathingly. 'I know the coverage normally given to these sort of things. They'll say a crash occurred earlier today in Monteraverde. Sixty—maybe seventy people were killed, among them six British tourists, and that will be that. Unless someone takes the trouble to find out details.'

Sister Teresa looked discomfited. 'But surely if you have a wife—a family—they would have taken the trouble to find out details?'

He sighed. 'If they knew I was travelling on that plane—perhaps! But what if they didn't know? What if I was working in Rio, and just taking a trip to La Paz? Would anyone know?'

Sister Teresa brightened. 'If you were working in Rio, then your employers would know you were missing.'

He frowned. 'Perhaps. Perhaps not.' He rubbed a hand across his forehead. It was beaded with perspiration, and he slumped a little against the pillows. The effort of trying to remember something—*anything*—was exhausting.

Sister Teresa came forward and shook his pillows firmly. 'This will not do, you know,' she said. 'Tiring yourself like this. Doctor Ramirez would be very angry if he knew.'

He turned his head away carelessly. He felt like saying to hell with Doctor Ramirez! It was *his* life that was brought to a standstill, and he had the right to try and recover the shredded membranes of his past.

But as suddenly as his anger had erupted it dispersed, and the sickening feeling of depression that always followed these unsuccessful attempts to recall his identity hovered on the brink of his consciousness. With grim determination he turned his attention to Sister Teresa, looking at her intently, deliberately causing the hot colour to flood her cheeks as she lifted his wrist to check his pulse rate.

'Tell me something,' he said in a low tone. 'What makes a girl like you turn to this kind of existence?'

'Please, senhor!' Sister Teresa dropped his wrist and shook out her thermometer, putting it under his tongue.

His eyes continued to appraise her as she bustled unnecessarily about the room, tidying his bedside table, folding the faded cotton bedspread more neatly at the foot of his bed, opening a window a couple of inches more.

'What are you afraid of?' he asked, when she was forced to return to the bed to read the thermometer. 'It was a simple question. Why can't you give a simple answer?'

'There is no simple answer, senhor.'

His eyes narrowed sardonically. 'That's no reply, Sister.'

'I cannot tell you what I do not know, senhor. It is what I wanted to do.' She moved towards the door 'Constancia will be here soon with your evening meal—'

'I'm not hungry. Don't go!' His eyes were appealing and she flushed again.

'I must.'

'Why? Are you afraid of me?' He half smiled. 'For all either of us knows, I might be a priest myself. We might have that in common.'

'I think not, senhor.'

'Why? Why not?'

Her fingers plucked nervously at her robe. 'You do not act like a priest, *senhor*.'

'How could I? I don't know who or what I am.'

'No—no, that is true. But there is something else. Something which is in your eyes—that makes me certain—'

His grey eyes mocked her. 'The way I look at you—is that it? As though I find you pleasing to my sight—'

'*Senhor*!' She was deeply disturbed now, and he suddenly felt remorse. He was using this innocent girl in an attempt to escape from the futility of his thoughts, and it was cruel when he knew she was powerless to defend herself.

'Oh, go!' he said abruptly. 'I'm sorry. I'm sorry if I've offended you.'

Sister Teresa hesitated uncertainly as though she would have liked to have said something more, but then with a little sigh she went out of the room, closing the door almost silently behind her.

With a muttered imprecation, he flung back the covers and thrust his legs out of bed, shivering a little as his feet encountered the chill bareness of the wooden floor. Straightening, he waited a moment for the throbbing in his head to subside after the unaccustomed exertion, and then walked slowly across to the window.

The view was quite startlingly magnificent, and he reflected dryly on the fact that ulcer-ridden businessmen would pay dearly for the opportunity to spend several weeks in such silent and dramatically beautiful surroundings

His mouth twisted. Now how had he known that? Was he so conversant with the business world, or was it merely supposition? Was he perhaps one of these ulcer-ridden businessmen himself? He pressed a hand against the lean muscles of his stomach. No; if he had had an ulcer Doctor Ramirez would have discovered it. His examinations were always infuriatingly thorough, and nothing so outstanding could have been missed.

He sighed, and took a deep breath of the mountain air. The hospital was built on the side of the mountain, and below them the valley sloped steeply away. A river tumbled riotously down the mountain side into the valley, gurgling and sucking its way between the moss-covered rocks and foliage. But the most majestic sight was towering above them—the high, snow-capped slopes of the mountain range that formed the backbone of the continent. The Andes, stark and ragged, beautiful from below and tortuous from above. He marvelled that anyone could have survived a plane crash among those peaks, and a sliver of remembered apprehension ran down his spine.

But closer at hand there were more domestic sights to be seen. The old man working on the slopes below, the jingling of goatbells on the early evening air. It was all so remote and peaceful, and he felt an unexpected release of tension. Standing here, seeing how simply these people accepted their lives, made him realise that there was something to be gained from every experience. Perhaps he was the fool, trying so desperately to pick up the threads of his life which must have been spent in the competitive world outside, constantly prey to the pressures of his fellow competitors.

He put his hands to his head as the throbbing began again. He could hear sounds in the passage outside his room now, and he guessed it was Constancia with his evening meal. He stumbled back to the bed just as the door opened and the elderly woman wheeled his trolley inside. She clicked her tongue when she saw he had been out of bed, chattering loudly in her own language, shaking her head as he got clumsily into bed, catching his toe in the long night-shirt which had been all Doctor Ramirez could produce for him to wear. He gritted his teeth and submitted silently to the incomprehensible rebukes she flung at him, despising himself for being unable to retaliate. But an immense weakness was overtaking him, and he sank back against the pillows wearily.

Constancia departed in a wave of indignation, and he picked disinterestedly at his food. The greasy stew on his plate was not appetising and he turned to the fruit, peeling a banana and biting into the flesh without enjoyment.

A few moments later the door of his room opened again and he looked up without surprise to see Doctor Ramirez on the threshold. He had guessed that Constancia would waste no time in reporting his misbehaviour.

Ramirez came slowly into the room, closing the door behind him. 'Now, *senhor*,' he said reproachfully. 'You know why I am here.'

'Of course. Constancia has told you I've been a naughty boy, and I must be punished.'

Ramirez shook his head. 'It is not like that at all, *senhor*. You do not suppose that I insist on bed rest for some nefarious purposes of my own, do you? Surely you realise that my actions are in your best interests—'

'Yes, yes, I know.' He moved his head restlessly on the pillow, ignoring the discomfort this caused him. 'Doctor Ramirez, I'm bored. Can't you understand that? *Bored*!' He lifted a hand and then let it fall against the coverlet. 'I've been here—how long? How many days? You don't seem to realise how long these days are becoming. I have nothing to read, I have no one to talk to. I just lie here and stare at the ceiling.'

'It is unfortunate, *senhor*, that there are no English books in the hospital. But I wish you would not become so morose. Your condition is improving daily. Already your temperature is almost normal. You are still weak, of course, but I think perhaps tomorrow you might be allowed to get up for a while and sit by the window—'

'When is something going to be done about finding out who I am?' He heaved a sigh.

'Things are being done, *senhor*. The authorities—'

'Oh, spare me that, at least!' He clenched his fists, and then the anger died out of his eyes as the ache in his head increased. 'Oh, damn this bloody pain—'

Ramirez bit his lip regretfully. '*Senhor*, if there was something I could do—some way in which I could help you recover your memory, I would not hesitate to try it. But I am powerless. There is nothing—no pressure on the brain—no possible reason why you should not recover your memory tomorrow. Believe me, *senhor*, I have seen cases like yours before. When your body is fit to take the strain, your memory will return, believe me!'

He had closed his eyes, but he opened them now and looked at the doctor. 'I know, I know,' he said quietly. 'I'm sorry. I know you're doing everything you can. I apologise.'

Ramirez spread his hands in a typically continental gesture. 'There is no need, *senhor*. I understand how you feel. But you will not get out of bed again without permission, will you? You might have fallen. You might have lain for several hours on the floor before you were discovered. Pneumonia is not among my plans for you.'

A faint smile crossed his face. 'Nor among mine, Doctor Ramirez.'

CHAPTER TWO

JUSTINA ALLOWED the mare to pick her own path down the mountain track. The horse was used to it, but Justina was not, and she was quite prepared to allow herself to go where the animal might take her. It was all so peaceful, so relaxing, after the taut atmosphere of the *castelo* and all the problems it represented, and she had deliberately lingered longer than she should with Luis and Morgana.

The faint breeze that stirred the massed ferns at the lakeside was cooler now, and the sun was sinking lower in the sky. She sighed, looking about her. Although it was three years since she had ridden here, it might have been only yesterday. Nothing changed, it all remained reassuringly familiar, and she wondered how she had existed so long in Andrew's artificial environment without either sight or sound of her homeland. This was where she belonged, and she had been a fool ever to imagine otherwise.

A frown marred the smoothness of her brow. In many ways it seemed more than three years since she left Monteraverde. Certainly she was more than three years older in experience. What an innocent she must have been to believe Andrew's protestations of undying passion when within three months of their marriage he had been making the same protestations to someone else. There was a tightness in her throat now as she remembered the humiliation of it all. She knew without Tia Renata's remonstrances she would have returned home, and abandoned any efforts to make their marriage work. But Tia Renata was a staunchly religious woman, and to her, the vows they had made were binding until death. She didn't want to hear about Andrew's infidelities. Just so long as Justina remained virtuous, and a good Catholic, that was all she seemed to care about.

Justina had had no one else to turn to. There had been Luis, of course. He was her cousin. But three years ago he had just been married himself, and newly elected *presidente* of Monteraverde. She could not bring herself to write to him of her troubles, even though she had known he would have helped her if he could.

Her parents were dead, killed in the uprising when she was a child, when Luis's father, then *presidente*, had been assassinated. It had been a terrible time. The dictator, Queras, had elected himself *presidente* and Justina had been sent, for safety, to live with her father's elderly aunt at the Castelo de la Roca.

And there she had stayed until at a reception given for the new *presidente* at the Palacio in Queranova, she had met Andrew Douglas.

The mare was on the flat of the valley floor now,

following the tumbling course of the river. Shading her eyes, Justina looked up to the towering peaks above her, noticing an eagle, wings outspread, soaring upward. There was something majestic about that swooping arc and she determinedly dug her heels into the animal's sides and urged it forward.

It was time she was back at the *castelo*. Tia Renata could have had another seizure while she was out. She should not have stayed away so long. But her mind ached with the effort of inventing excuses why Andrew had not yet arrived, and sooner or later her aunt was bound to suspect the truth. And then...

She looked down at her hands, at the broad, faceted band of her wedding ring. She longed to remove it, to destroy for ever the shabby traces of a marriage which had been no marriage at all, but she could not. So long as Tia Renata lived, she had to pretend that Andrew was still her husband—while Andrew was *dead*!

Her heart pounded heavily. Things had a habit of happening suddenly. For a long time nothing seemed to happen; nothing out of the ordinary, that is. And then, without warning, the pattern of one's life is shattered so completely that one wonders how it can have existed so long.

It would be futile to pretend remorse at Andrew's death. She did not love him then, and she doubted whether she had ever done so. Surely love could not die so quickly, so completely, leaving no trace of itself behind. What she had felt for Andrew had been her first initiation into the attraction between the sexes. If she had been older, more experienced, she would have seen it for what it was, but she had lived so long in Tia Renata's secluded *castelo* that she had been instantly overwhelmed by the attentions of an attractive man. And Andrew had been attractive, there could be no doubt of that, and he had been experienced enough to know exactly the right approach to use to infatuate Justina.

She tucked a strand of chestnut gold hair behind one small ear. How stupid she had been! How utterly ripe for disillusion! And disillusionment had come more quickly than she could ever have thought possible—on her wedding night, in fact.

Her cheeks burned as she remembered the humiliation of that ungentle consummation of their marriage. Andrew had been drinking, a usual habit with him, she was to find, except when he was racing and his own life was put in the balance, and he had been sufficiently drunk to care little that Justina was not one of the experienced socialites he was used to having affairs with. When it was over, and Justina lay with tear-wet cheeks, Andrew turned on his side and fell into a noisy slumber, indifferent to her distress.

It was a rude awakening from innocence for the girl brought up by her aunt and educated at the Convent of the Assumption, and Justina had never again

been able to suffer Andrew touching her without
freezing up inside.

Maybe she had been partially to blame for the di
saster of their marriage. Maybe she had expected too
much of him. She didn't know enough about men to
know whether Andrew's behaviour was typical. He
had accused her of being frigid, and she had had to
accept that he was right. She did not enjoy his attentions, and was grateful when he began to leave her
alone. And now she was thankful there had been no
children. She wanted nothing left to remind her of her
folly.

The Castelo de la Roca was situated at the end of
the valley. Built of local stone, it blended well with
the rocky hillside into which it had been hewn, its
grey walls a continuation of the rock face. Although
it was termed a castle, it was small and compact, only
its turreted roofs and thick walls giving any truth to
the description.

Justina allowed the mare to climb the stony path to
the gates and entered through them into a small courtyard. A servant took her horse and she entered the
building through a studded wooden door.

The hall of the *castelo* was square and compact,
not at all the spacious apartment one would have expected in a building such as this, with only a spiral
stairway leading to the upper floor. An arched entrance led through to a large lounge which overlooked
the sweep of the valley, and here a fire burned even

on the hottest day. The walls of the *castelo* were very thick and repelled heat. The lounge was a comfortable room, its polished floor strewn with skin rugs, its walls lined with tapestries depicting the turbulent history of the country.

Juana Mateo, her aunt's elderly companion, was sitting in the lounge, beneath the windows, sewing. She seemed to spend her days sewing and Justina marvelled that her eyes required no aid to perform such intricate and delicate work. She looked up at Justina's entrance, and smiled politely. She had been employed after Justina's marriage as companion to her aunt, and Justina was aware that she was anxious now about her own future. If Renata de la Roca should die...

'You have been a long time, *senhora*,' she said. 'I was becoming concerned about you.'

Justina threw her riding gloves on to the table to one side of the huge fireplace, and shrugged. Juana's demeanour did not suggest anxiety, but then she might be doing her an injustice.

'I stayed longer than I intended with Luis and Morgana,' she answered. 'It's so long since I've seen them, and we had so much to talk about.'

Juana nodded her head slowly. 'You aunt has been sleeping. The nurse is sitting with her now. Perhaps you should go and see whether she has been asking for you.'

Justina hesitated. 'How do you think my aunt is,

Juana? I mean—do you think she's making any improvement?'

Juana looked up, frowning. 'Since you ask, *senhora*, yes, yes, I do. But have you some reason for asking such a question? Surely you do not intend returning to Europe immed—'

'*No!*' Justina interrupted her hotly. 'No.' She coloured. The last thing she wanted was for anyone to think she might consider returning to Europe. So far as she was concerned that phase of her life was over—for good. 'I—I—naturally you're more used to her than I am. I thought you would know if there was an improvement...'

Juana studied the girl thoughtfully. 'Is something troubling you then, *senhora*? You look—concerned.'

Justina turned away, making a dismissive gesture. 'There's nothing the matter with me,' she denied.

'I thought—seeing that your husband has not arrived—you might be concerned about him,' murmured Juana insinuatively.

Justina bent her head. She dared not let Juana see the anxiety in her eyes. 'An—Andrew will be here—eventually,' she said. 'Excuse me. I'll go and see how my aunt is for myself.'

As she ran up the stairs, her heart was thumping uncomfortably loudly. Even Juana was becoming suspicious. And if her aunt was improving she would demand to know why Andrew was not here. But how could she tell Tia Renata that Andrew was dead after what the solicitor had told her? The *castelo* was her home, her refuge against the outside world, and she dared not place that in jeopardy, not now, not after everything that had happened.

The terrible fluttery sensation of nerves which had become such an accepted part of her metabolism started up again, and she felt almost physically sick.

The first floor landing ran in two directions and all the main bedrooms opened on to this one corridor. Her aunt's room was the master bedroom, an enormous apartment, which used to terrify her when she was a child. But now there was an aura of medication about it, and the windows were shuttered against the brilliance of the afternoon sun.

The nurse was seated by her aunt's bed. She was a woman of about thirty, dark and efficient, very correct in her starched uniform. She rose to her feet as Justina entered, and a faint smile touched her lips.

'Good evening, *senhora*,' she said. 'Did you enjoy your ride?'

'Thank you, yes.' Justina's gaze flickered to the figure in the bed. 'How is my aunt?'

The nurse turned and surveyed her patient. Renata de la Roca had never been a woman of great stature, and now her illness had fined her flesh down to the minimum, and she looked very fragile. But for all that, Justina knew that once her eyes opened the dominant spirit which kept her alive would be visible once more.

'Your aunt has been sleeping most of the afternoon, *senhora*,' Nurse Gomez replied. 'But I think there has been some slight improvement in her breathing.'

Justina bit her lip, and then smiled. 'You must be tired, sitting here all afternoon. Go down to Benita and have something to eat and drink. I will stay with my aunt.'

Nurse Gomez hesitated. 'They will bring me a tray, *senhora*.'

'Nevertheless, you would enjoy a break, would you not?'

The nurse smiled reluctantly. 'Naturally I would, *senhora*.'

'Very well then, go.' Justina seated herself in the chair beside her aunt's bed. 'I shall have plenty of time to bathe before the evening meal when you return, yes?'

Nurse Gomez nodded. 'You're very kind, *senhora*.'

Justina shook her head, and the nurse left her, closing the door silently behind her. After she had gone, Justina shifted more comfortably in her chair and looked towards the shuttered windows. From here it was possible to view the whole length of the valley, but now, with the shutters closed, the room was dim and cool.

She looked at the old lady in the bed. For all the brilliance of her aunt's gaze when she was awake, she was almost blind now and her hearing was not what it should be. And after all, how could it be? She was eighty years old. A great age for someone who had lived such a cloistered life. Renata had never married, and Justina sometimes wondered whether there had ever been a man in her aunt's life.

The old lady stirred and said something unintelligible and Justina started. But her aunt was not awake. She seemed to be talking in her sleep, her fingers plucking jerkily at the coverlet. Justina glanced towards the closed door of the room and wondered whether she ought to call back the nurse. Was her aunt delirious? Was she in pain? Or was she merely restless?

Renata became still again, and Justina relaxed. She was abnormally sensitive to anxiety, and after the exhausting sleepless nights following Andrew's accident, her nerves were as taut as violin strings.

Her aunt stirred once more and Justina bent towards her. Renata seemed to be wanting to say something, and her gnarled fingers groped urgently across the coverlet, fastening themselves round Justina's slim wrist.

'Shouldn't…shouldn't…have let her go…' Renata whispered breathily, and Justina shook her head.

'Shouldn't have let who go, Tia Renata?' she asked gently.

But Renata didn't seem to hear her. 'Shouldn't… shouldn't have done it…knew it wouldn't work out.' The old lady moved her head slowly from side to side.

'What wouldn't work out, Tia Renata?' Justina gave a helpless little movement of her shoulders. Whatever it was that was troubling her aunt, was interrupting her rest.

'Should—should have taken Reverend Mother's advice…should have let her talk to…to… Justina…' Her voice faded away, and Justina shivered involuntarily. Renata's fingers relaxed then, and she was able to draw her wrist away. She sank back in her chair, rubbing her wrist absently, her mind tormented by what she had just heard. What did it all mean? Why was her aunt troubled about letting her, Justina, go? But where? What was she talking about?

She was still puzzling over what her aunt had said when Nurse Gomez returned. The nurse smiled gratefully at her.

'That was very kind of you, *senhora*,' she said. 'I went outside and ate my meal there. It was so cool and pleasant in the early evening air.'

Justina shook her head, managing to act naturally. 'That's all right. I'll do it again tomorrow. It's only right that you should have some free time.'

'I am paid to be always available,' explained the nurse, apologetically. 'I don't mind really.'

Justina walked towards the door. 'I must go. I'll see you later.'

The nurse nodded and smiled again, and Justina went out and stood for a moment on the landing, her thoughts confused. Then, slowly, she went downstairs again.

Juana Mateo was still sitting in the lounge sewing, but Justina saw at once that she had changed her dress. She looked up as Justina entered the room and her eyes narrowed at the thoughtful expression on the girl's face.

'Is something wrong, *senhora*?' she queried. And then quickly: 'It's not your aunt, is it? She has not had another attack—'

'No, no, nothing like that.' Justina shook her head. 'She's still sleeping.'

'I see,' Juana nodded. 'That is good. But you look tired, *senhora*. Are you sure nothing is troubling you?'

Justina flung herself into a chair. 'Why should anything be troubling me? Apart from Tia Renata's health, of course.'

Juana put her sewing aside, and folded her hands in her lap. 'Are you sure you are not concerned about your husband, *senhora*?'

Justina pressed her lips together, drumming her fingers impatiently against the surface of an occasional table by her chair. 'I've already told you, Juana. Andrew will be here soon.'

Juana studied the girl thoughtfully. 'I do not think your aunt thinks so, *senhora*,' she said quietly, startling Justina into immobility.

'What do you mean?'

Juana sighed. 'Perhaps I should not have said that—'

'But you have said it, Juana. What do you mean by it?'

Juana looked down at her hands. 'Your aunt has been worried about you, *senhora*. She is afraid you are not happy with this Englishman.'

'What?' Justina could hardly believe her ears. Tia Renata must know that she had never been actually *happy* with Andrew. Heavens, when she recalled those letters she had written to her aunt, begging her to let her come home...

Juana went on: 'It is true. Since her health began to deteriorate at the beginning of the year, she has become increasingly concerned about your marriage. She is afraid that if anything were to happen to her, you might leave this Englishman, break up your marriage, break your vows...'

Justina sat up in her seat. 'And?' she added tremulously.

Juana shrugged. 'You know your aunt could never accept that.'

Justina opened her mouth to protest and then closed it again. Short of revealing her own feelings in the matter there was little she could say. She could only wait, and ask questions, and try to understand her aunt's reasoning.

Now she bent her head, digging her nails into the

palm of her hand. 'My aunt wanted me to marry—Andrew.'

'I know. But now she thinks perhaps it would have been better that you did not.'

Justina was confused. 'You mean—she had other plans for me?'

Juana rose to her feet. 'I have been told you were an excellent pupil at the convent. There were times when it was perhaps hoped...that you...'

'That I might take orders? Enter the convent as a novice?' Justina was horrified. Never at any time had she felt the calling of such a life.

Juana shrugged. 'It is possible.'

At that moment Benita, the housekeeper, appeared at the entrance to the lounge. 'What time would you like to eat, *senhora*?' she enquired of Justina.

Justina dragged her thoughts back to the immediate present with difficulty and glanced at the broad, masculine watch encircling her narrow wrist. 'Oh, in say—half an hour, Benita, please. Is that all right?'

The housekeeper nodded her acquiescence and withdrew and Justina got determinedly to her feet. 'I must shower and change, Juana,' she said, excusing herself, and crossed the hall to mount the stairs to her room with absent slowness. The events of the past hour had put her mind in a turmoil and she needed time to assimilate her position.

Juana's words had given her a vague insight into the workings of her aunt's mind, and she did not care to speculate on what might happen when Renata discovered that Andrew was dead...

Later, bathed and changed into a long apricot velvet caftan, her long hair loose about her shoulders, she went downstairs to join Juana for their evening meal. But surprisingly, the elderly companion was not alone. A tall dark man, past middle age, dressed in the garb of a priest, was standing in the lounge talking to Juana, and Justina's eyes brightened perceptibly.

'Father Juan!' she exclaimed, with pleasure. 'Oh, it is good to see you!'

The man turned and took Justina's outstretched hands warmly. '*Que*, but what is this?' he queried teasingly. 'Can this really be little Justina? You seem so—so soignée!'

Justina's lips tilted at the corners. 'Why, thank you, Father. You're looking well. You're going to stay and eat with us, of course.'

Father Juan inclined his head. 'That was my intention, if you'll have me.' He smiled, and Justina relaxed. She had not been looking forward to this evening alone with Juana after their conversation earlier, and besides, Father Juan was one of her favourite people. It would be marvellous to talk to him again. He was Luis's uncle, as well as being a close friend of Tia Renata's.

During the meal they talked about her aunt. Father Juan was anxious about her and voiced his doubts about the completeness of her eventual recovery.

'Your aunt is old and frail, Justina,' he said, shaking his head regretfully. 'It is possible that another attack like the last one could kill her. You must be prepared for this. It is well that you have a husband to turn to, or you would be completely alone and at the mercy of fortune-hunters.'

Justina bent her head, studying the amber wine in her glass, holding the delicate crystal container between her fingers. 'Doctor Ramirez is hopeful that the new drug he is using will strengthen her condition,' she said.

Father Juan lifted his shoulders in an eloquent gesture. 'Drugs can only do so much, Justina. Do not place too much faith in such things. Your aunt has had a good life, she has reached old age without experiencing any of the discomforts of life. Be thankful for that.'

'Of course, Father.' Justina instilled a note of brightness into her voice. Surveying him through the dark fringe of her lashes, she said: 'And you must know how grateful my aunt is for your friendship and encouragement, particularly at this time.'

Father Juan wiped his mouth on his napkin. 'That may be so, Justina. But nevertheless, it is you whom Renata needs most.'

Justina tipped her head to one side. 'Is it?'

'Of course.' He shook his head. 'It will be better when your husband is here to support you. Your future happiness is your aunt's greatest concern at the moment.'

Justina glanced uncomfortably at Juana. Sooner or later the conversation always seemed to come round to Andrew. And why not? It was the most natural thing in the world that everyone should be concerned about the whereabouts of her husband. Only *she* was sensitive to such comments.

Replacing her glass on the table, she wondered how she had got herself into this invidious position. She supposed it had begun at the airport in Queranova when she was met from the plane by Sergio Manuelo, her aunt's solicitor. He had taken little time to explain that her aunt was dying, that she could take no sudden shocks, that she was eager to see Justina and her husband before she died to be sure that Justina was content.

Justina, already in a state of shock from Andrew's accident, had listened and said nothing. She had not mentioned that she was a widow, that her husband would not be following on, she had remained silent, and by so doing, she had committed herself to perjury.

But this was her greatest test. Lying to the solicitor was one thing. Lying to Father Juan, her confessor, was quite another.

Getting to her feet, she walked across to the cocktail cabinet in the corner of the room. 'May I offer you a liqueur, Father?' she asked, and Father Juan was temporarily diverted.

Later, over coffee, Justina tried to introduce another topic of conversation. 'I must go up to the convent,' she said. 'I'd like to see Sister Sofia and Sister Teresa again. And Reverend Mother, of course.'

Father Juan nodded benignly. 'And I'm sure they would be delighted to see you, my child. Although, Sister Teresa is working at the mission hospital now.'

Justina poured more coffee into her cup. 'And does she like the work? I remember she did say she wanted to take up nursing.'

Father Juan raised his dark eyebrows. 'I think she is happy. Sometimes I wonder, though, whether she is entirely suited to such a life.'

'Why do you say that?'

Father Juan frowned. 'Perhaps I am being unkind. Sister Teresa is a dedicated nurse. But there is a man at the hospital at the moment, and I am afraid...' His voice trailed away for a moment. Then he went on: 'Perhaps you have heard of this patient, Justina. He was the sole survivor of that terrible plane crash in the mountains a couple of weeks ago. Just after you arrived here, in fact.'

Justina was interested. 'I don't remember anything about it. But then Tia Renata has been so ill...'

'Of course,' Father Juan nodded. 'No doubt the news was of little importance to you at that time. But anyway, this man is there, and unfortunately he has lost his memory.'

Justina looked up sharply. 'Lost his memory?'

'Yes.' Father Juan sipped his coffee thoughtfully. 'They had some difficulty at first because he is English, but your friend Sister Teresa was able to ease the situation. Ramirez says his amnesia is only a temporary condition, but it is two weeks now and there has been no significant recovery. I am afraid they are beginning to lose hope.'

Justina quivered. The weirdest sensations were running through her, and she felt an intense curiosity about this unknown Englishman. 'You say—no one knows his identity?' she queried.

'No, no one. These things take time, as you know, and it is not a simple investigation. The remains of the aircraft and the identity of the other passengers have been difficult to find, and there has been no successful enquiry about this man.'

'I—see.' Justina wet her dry lips with her tongue. Crazy, unformed ideas were running through her brain, and she could hardly concentrate on what she was doing. Father Juan had spoken to her twice before she realised he was saying something else.

'Perhaps they will allow you to see him, Justina. After all, you are newly out from England yourself. You may be able to talk to him about his country— you may alert some spark of recognition inside him— who knows? And in any case, I am sure he would be glad to speak with someone who understands his language fluently.'

Justina nodded. 'If—if you think it would serve some useful purpose, Father, of course I'll go.'

Father Juan shrugged. 'I confess my motives are not wholly concerned with the patient. I would prefer Sister Teresa to have less to do with this man. I feel he is a disturbing influence upon her.'

Justina helped herself to a cigarette and lit it, inhaling deeply. She didn't often smoke. It was one of the habits Andrew had practically forced upon her. But there were times when the soporific exhalation of smoke into the air had a soothing effect on her nerves, and this was one of those times.

Her mind buzzed with thoughts and speculations, and she would have liked to have questioned Father Juan more closely about this man before she saw him for herself. But she could hardly do so without arousing his curiosity, and she knew the scarcely acceptable ideas which had invaded her consciousness since she learnt of this man's existence could only realise themselves spontaneously. If he was to be of any use to her, the decision must be made before she left for the mission.

Before he left, Father Juan went again to see her aunt. Justina accompanied him. Renata was awake now, looking pale and hollow-eyed against her pillows. Her sight was deteriorating rapidly, and although she knew when someone was there, she could not distinguish features.

She welcomed the priest warmly, and he sat on the side of her bed, holding her thin hands in his, telling her how delighted he was to hear that she was recovering.

Renata looked beyond him to where Justina stood at the foot of the bed. 'It is good to have Justina back again,' she said. 'I did not realise how much I had missed her.'

Father Juan glanced round at the girl and nodded. 'Yes. Your niece has grown into quite a beautiful young woman. She has—matured. Yes, that is the word—matured.'

'You think she is happy, Juan?' Renata's voice was husky, and Justina stiffened.

'Oh, yes, I think so,' Father Juan replied slowly. 'Do not concern yourself, Renata. Justina is your niece. She will be all right.'

Renata shook her head doubtfully, her breathing a little faster. 'I am afraid for her, Juan. She is not like me. How could she be? I am a hardened old woman, hardened by the tragedies of death and revolution. I have seen my friends killed for nothing except their beliefs; Justina's own parents, imprisoned and tortured for loving their *presidente*. Justina has seen none of this. She has been shielded, protected—all her life—'

'But Monteraverde is a peaceful country now, Renata.' Father Juan squeezed her fingers. 'Revolutions are a thing of the past. There is no reason why Justina's children—her grandchildren—should not live in peace here!'

'That has been said before, Juan.'

'You're living in the past, Renata.'

'Perhaps I am, perhaps I am. Tell me...' She looked towards her niece. 'When will Andrew be here?'

Justina felt the hot colour burning her cheeks once more and prayed that Father Juan would not notice. 'Soon, Tia Renata, soon,' she said quickly, and turned away towards the windows. She hated this—the lies—the deceit. But if she told the truth now...

Father Juan seemed to notice nothing amiss, for he rose from the bed and said: 'And now I must go. It is getting late, and you must get plenty of rest. But I am staying in the valley, Renata, and I will come again soon.'

'Oh, do!' Renata clung to his hands. 'I—I need your strength, Juan.'

'God will give you strength, my dear,' murmured Father Juan softly, leaning towards her to give her a blessing before he left.

Downstairs he put his hands on Justina's shoulders as they stood together in the hall. 'I will tell Doctor Ramirez that you will be visiting the mission. When shall I say you will come? Tomorrow? The day after?'

Justina hesitated. Even now there was no definite

decision in her mind, and she pondered the advisability of making the situation more complex than it
already was. With a faint sigh, she said.

'Probably in two days, Father. I—well, I'm not sure
about tomorrow.'

'Very well.' He frowned. 'And if you do not wish
to see this man, it is not essential that you should do
so.'

'I—I haven't given the matter a lot of thought,' she
temporised. 'It's been wonderful seeing you again,
Father. You must come again—and soon. You know
you're always welcome.'

'Thank you, my child.' Father Juan paused in the
heavy entrance. 'It is good to know that your life in
England has not altered your personality.'

Justina closed the door and leaned back against it
after he had gone. There was an immense weight of
anxiety on her shoulders, combined with an undeni-
able feeling of guilt. It was true she had made no
definite decision yet; it was true that the idea of claiming this unknown man as her husband was still only
a crazy thought motivated by the desire to extract
herself once and for all from any plans Tia Renata
might have for her; and yet the guilt was there because having committed herself so far she was being
compelled to commit herself further...

CHAPTER THREE

ANTONIO RAMIREZ had brought him some clothes.

As well as underclothing, there were a couple of navy knitted cotton shirts which laced to the neckline, and close-fitting cream denim trousers. There was also a chunky cream sweater for cooler evenings. The casual attire suited his lean, muscular body and he wondered, rather wryly, what age he might be.

Ramirez had brought him a razor, and he had taken great pleasure in shaving away the growth of beard, leaving only sideburns to darken his jawline. His hair needed cutting, but as it was inclined to curl where it touched his collar, it did not look at all bad.

For the past few days they had been allowing him time out of bed, and he had even gone so far as to don a dressing gown and walk in the garden of the mission hospital. The white-robed Sisters smiled on his increasing activity, whispering together behind their hands as he passed, making him intensely aware of his masculinity in this almost wholly feminine atmosphere.

It was also becoming obvious that as his general health improved he could not continue to remain a burden on the already overworked Sisters. Had he been in England, it would have been a comparatively simple matter to contact some organisation who would have done their utmost to help him, but here, miles from that kind of civilisation, in a country where plumbing of any kind was considered a luxury, it was rather more difficult.

Apart from anything else, he didn't know how he had earned a living before the plane crash. When he tried to bring any occupation to mind there was just a blank, and although Ramirez had produced several textbooks, they were mostly written in Portuguese and conveyed nothing to him. Once, when he saw some written figures, he thought he felt a vague recognition, and he wondered if he might be a teacher of some sort, but the feeling left him as soon as he attempted to put it to the test.

The blind panic which had occasionally gripped him when he considered that he might never regain his memory was not so frequent now, and he thought, rather grimly, that sooner or later the mind adapted itself to anything. The depression, too, was not so overwhelming, and it was almost frightening to realise that his mind might have decided not to try so hard any more. Was that possible? Could one's personality be wiped out so completely?

In the mornings he usually had coffee with Antonio Ramirez on the verandah of the small mission hospital. He had discovered he, too, enjoyed the cheroots

Antonio smoked, and this was the time of day he found most acceptable.

They were sitting on the verandah as usual one morning when two people on horseback came into view, lower down the winding, mud-baked track. From the verandah, it was possible to see far down into the valley, and in other circumstances he might have found the whole episode rather enjoyable. The sun beat down on the fronded roof of their shelter, and the air was warm and spiced with the scents of the herbs which the Sisters grew in the hospital grounds.

As the riders drew nearer, he could see that one of them was a young woman. Long, dark gold hair showed beneath the broad-brimmed sombrero she was wearing to protect her head from the sun, while the casual attire of brown suede pants and open-necked lemon shirt accentuated her intense femininity. The full curve of her breast rose and fell beneath the buttoned shirt, while the long slender length of her legs was enhanced by the masculine garb. There was a boy with her, little more than fifteen or sixteen years of age, and he guessed, correctly as it happened, that he was merely her escort.

Doctor Ramirez rose as they cantered up to the verandah rail and he did likewise, but what neither of them was prepared for was the sudden exclamation which sprang from the girl's lips as she slid down from her horse. Her face seemed to pale slightly, and then, without even looking at the doctor, she leapt up the steps to confront him, excitedly.

'*Mãe de deus*!' she cried, grasping his forearms with her hands. 'Can it be true? Is it you, Andrew! Oh, *por amor de Deus*, what does this mean?'

There was a moment when they all seemed transfixed, when only that faint breeze which stirred the fronds of the cool verandah made its own gentle whispering, and they might have been turned to stone.

And then Ramirez seemed to come to life, and said, in a strangled tone: 'Justina, you can't mean that this man is your husband!'

The girl was nodding, slowly and disbelievingly. 'That—that is exactly what I do mean!' she uttered breathlessly. 'This—this man is Andrew Douglas— my husband!'

He was amazed, astounded, even vaguely troubled. On those rare occasions when he had pictured someone turning up who could identify him he had felt sure he would feel some sense of recognition, of kinship, perhaps; at any rate he had consoled his imagination with such beliefs. And yet now here was this young woman, this *alien* young woman, for from her accent it was obvious she was Monteraverdian, claiming that not only did she know him and could put a name to him, but that he was her *husband*! It was unbelievable, incredible, *fantastic*!

Could it be so? Could this girl—this *Justina*, as

Ramirez had called her, know him so intimately? Had she really shared his life, his home, his *bed*? Had they been married long? She scarcely looked old enough to be married at all. Had they any children? It was absolutely crazy—and he couldn't accept it.

Ramirez seemed to sense that his erstwhile patient's health was not being improved by standing here on the verandah of the hospital with the sun increasing in heat by the minute undergoing the most rigorous type of mental strain. Whether or not he was Justina's husband was immaterial at this moment. What was important was that he should not overtax the strength which was only now returning.

'Come,' he said. 'We will go inside. We cannot discuss this here.'

Justina preceded them both into the small reception hall of the hospital, and then Ramirez went ahead, leading the way into his office. Venetian blinds shaded the slatted bands of sunshine here, and there were two comfortable chairs which the doctor indicated they should both use.

He sat down rather thankfully after Justina had subsided into Ramirez's chair. He still felt physically stunned, and he was finding it difficult to voice the thousand and one questions that sprang to his tired brain.

Justina seemed to have no such misgivings, for she was regarding him intently, her wide brown eyes warm and friendly. He shook his head a trifle resignedly. What had he expected to find in her eyes? Not exactly what he was seeing. Shouldn't there be something more than friendship there if their marriage was a happy one? And why had he been on that plane—alone?

He tried to hold her gaze with his, endeavouring to summon up some kind of intimacy between them, but almost at once she looked away, her eyes darting swiftly to Ramirez's face.

He frowned, and a twinge of apprehension touched him. What if the girl was lying? What if she had some other purpose for claiming him as her husband? He was a stranger, in a strange land, and she could be anybody. It was debatable whether it was better to remain in ignorance of one's identity if one could not feel any association whatsoever with whoever it was who identified one.

Ramirez perched on the corner of his desk and looked down into Justina's eyes. 'Now slowly, Justina,' he said. 'Apart from the fact that this man must look like your husband, what makes you think so certainly that my patient is who you say he is?'

Justina took a deep breath. 'As—as you know, I've been—expecting Andrew to arrive—to follow me here.'

'Yes. Your aunt told me.'

'Well, he—hasn't arrived. Even though—I've heard from friends that he left England. I—I imagined something must have delayed him. We—don't correspond. And—and my aunt has been so ill—'

'I see.' Ramirez frowned. 'And you think Andrew might have been on this plane, flying to La Paz?'

'It's possible. He—well, he would fly into Rio, wouldn't he? He might have decided to fly on to Bolivia and drive over the border into the valley, rather than wait for a flight to Queranova.'

Doctor Ramirez bit his lip. 'It's possible, I suppose, Justina. But highly unlikely, I would say.'

Justina flushed. 'How can you say that? When I can see Andrew sitting there in front of me! It's the most reasonable explanation.'

Doctor Ramirez slid down off the desk. 'Very well,' he said, folding his arms. 'Suppose we accept that the supposition is possible. Let us go on from there. What else can you tell me about your husband? Does he have any distinguishing marks? Any condition which might be identifiable?'

Justina shook her head slowly. 'I don't think so.'

'You don't *think* so?' Ramirez placed his hands, palms downward, on the desk. 'Justina, do you have any idea what you are saying? You are claiming this man to be your husband, simply because his facial characteristics would appear to be the same as your husband's.'

Justina rose to her feet now, thrusting back the swathe of heavy hair from her face. 'You're forgetting the circumstances,' she cried. 'You must admit, it is quite a coincidence.'

'Will the pair of you stop behaving as though I'm no longer present?' he demanded sharply. 'Don't I have any say in the matter? It is my future you're discussing, isn't it?'

Doctor Ramirez turned to him apologetically. 'Of course, *senhor*, you must forgive us. But this situation is a new one for me. I am completely in the dark. Not that the most expert of my colleagues can give any actual explanation for this condition, but I must be absolutely certain that Justina's claim is in your best interests.'

He raked his long fingers through the thick darkness of his hair, and closed his eyes in momentary frustration. The whole thing was assuming the proportions of some kind of farcical comedy of errors, and he no longer had any desire to be the principal player.

'Look, Ramirez,' he said abruptly. 'Can't we assume at least that there might be some truth in what this young woman says? In any event, it's worth a try. Maybe if I were to see our home—meet other people who know who I am—'

'*No!*' The girl uttered the word almost before he had finished speaking. 'No, that's not possible—Andrew. We—our home is not in Monteraverde. We— lived in England, don't you remember? There—

there's no one here who can identify you—except my aunt, of course—'

'And she's partially blind,' finished Ramirez dryly.

'I see.' He looked towards Justina. 'Tell me about myself. Tell me what kind of occupation I follow— how I earn my living. Do we have a family?'

Justina shook her head. 'No, no family.' She wetted her lips with her tongue, seeming to study what to say next. His suspicions of her authenticity increased. 'You—you're a racing driver. You don't have a regular job. There—there's no need. Your father was Sir David Douglas, and he left you well provided for.'

'I see.' He frowned, tugging absently at the lobe of his ear. 'Go on. None of this means a thing to me so far. How long have we been married? How old am I? Where did we meet?'

Justina hesitated. 'We met at a reception in Queranova. The—the new *presidente* had just been elected, and as I am his cousin, I was there.'

'Wait a minute! Do I know this—this *presidente*?' Ramirez's eyes widened. 'Yes, Justina—Luis would know him.'

Justina twisted her hands together. 'I—I suppose so. But when I was talking to Luis a few days ago, I understood he was returning to Queranova almost immediately. He—he and Morgana.'

'*Condenacao*!' Ramirez snapped his fingers impatiently.

'Well, never mind that right now. Go on about the other matters. Please!'

Justina pressed a hand to her throat. 'Very well. Now what else was there? Oh, yes—we've been married a little over three years and your age is—thirty-seven.'

'Quite a lot older than you, then,' he observed dryly.

'Y—yes. I'm—I'm not yet twenty-two.'

'I see.'

He drew his brows together in painful concentration. For God's sake, some of this should have meant something to him—but it didn't. She might have been talking about a complete stranger for all the affinity he felt to this man's identity. *A racing driver!* Was it possible? He couldn't imagine himself following such a useless occupation. During the time he had been here at the mission hospital, he had come to admire and respect Antonio Ramirez and what he was trying to do. Surely he would not be content with racing cars for a living! Surely the intelligence he felt certain he possessed needed a useful outlet. Whenever he had tried to remember his occupation it had always been in terms of industry or education; never the kind of career that was constantly in the public eye. He couldn't be absolutely sure, of course, but he couldn't see himself as a public figure, reacting to the adulation of the masses.

Ramirez lifted the box of cheroots off his desk and

handed one to him. 'Here,' he said, shaking his head. 'Relax! There is no point in plaguing your brain like this. When the time comes for your memory to return, it will return, believe me.'

Justina glanced at the doctor. 'And—and when is that likely to be, Doctor?' she enquired, rather quickly.

Ramirez shrugged. 'Who knows?'

'What Doctor Ramirez is trying to say is that he has absolutely no idea whether I ever will regain my memory.' He drew deeply on the cheroot. 'Do you want to be stuck, possibly for life, with a man who can't even recollect your face?'

Justina made a deprecatory movement of her hand. 'Please, don't speak like this. As Doctor Ramirez says—when the time is right your memory will return.'

'And what if it does not?' His lips twisted.

Ramirez walked round his desk. 'Let us assume for the moment that my patient is your husband. Are there not enquiries that can be made by the airline company and by your friends or authorised representatives in England that would settle this matter one way or the other?'

Justina subsided into her chair again. 'Of course,' she said, and he was struck again by the vaguely nervous expression that invaded her eyes whenever she was confronted by statements like these. Was he imagining things, or was she really doubtful of putting his identity to the test? Was she prepared to accept him on face value without delving into all the circumstances? And if so—why? It was puzzling, but he already had enough puzzles of his own to deal with without conjuring up more. For the moment the initiative was out of his hands, and his most sensible course of action would be to drift with the tide, be directed in whatever direction Ramirez thought best, and wait for some tangible evidence of his character to appear.

'Very well then,' Ramirez was saying now. 'You will appreciate, Justina, that I need to be absolutely sure my patient is who you say he is before I can allow you to remove him from the clinic. I could not authorise such a course of action without actual proof.'

The girl's cheeks paled slightly. 'I see,' she said, and he could tell she was disturbed by this news. He wondered what she would do now. Could she produce the proof Ramirez needed? And if so—when?

Ramirez hesitated a moment and then walked towards the door. 'I think we could all use a drink,' he commented dryly. 'You will excuse me if I leave you two alone for a few moments, won't you?' He looked at his patient. 'Your first visitor, *senhor*. It is quite an occasion, is it not?'

After the door had closed behind the doctor, he rose to his feet, walking restlessly about the room. It had been easy to be speculative and casual under Ramirez's clinical gaze, but without him the situation altered rapidly. If what this girl—this Justina—said was true, then he should take this opportunity to put it to the test.

He halted before the girl, looking down at her curiously. 'Your name?' he said. 'Before you took—my name, that is. What was it?'

'De—de la Roca,' she said jerkily.

'Justina de la Roca!' He said the words aloud to himself. 'No. It means nothing to me.' He frowned, studying her intently: 'Why was I following you to Monteraverde? Because your aunt is ill?'

'Y—yes. I—I had a telegram. Don—don't you remember?'

He gave a derisory grimace. 'Oh, yes, of course. I forgot everything else, but I remember the telegram.'

Her lips parted involuntarily, and then she coloured at the mocking glint in his eyes. 'I'm—I'm sorry,' she said.

He hooked his thumbs into the belt of his trousers. In spite of the incongruity of their situation he found her a very attractive young woman, and he thought rather wryly that it might prove something to Ramirez to know that at least she seemed to be the type of woman he could feel attracted to.

On impulse, he put out a hand and fingered the silken curtain of hair that fell past her shoulders, but she flinched away from his touch like a deer that is startled into flight by some unexpected action. He allowed his hand to fall to his side at once, but he wondered impatiently why she should have reacted like that. Dear God, if she was his wife, he had a right to touch her, didn't he? Or was the situation between them not all it might be? Was their marriage floundering? Was that why she had flown all the way to South America alone? Surely he should have accompanied her if her aunt was so seriously ill.

He drew his brows together, rubbing his temples impotently. *If only he could remember!*

And then he did recall something. It was only a fleeting glimpse, and yet for a moment the idea of their marriage being on the rocks rang true. It was as though a door had opened a couple of inches allowing him a brief impression of arguments and rows culminating in—what? That he could not recall.

He was about to tell her, and then he decided against it. There was no point in raising hopes unnecessarily, and besides, if their marriage had been crumbling that was one aspect that might be improved by remaining silent. So he said nothing, and she seemed relieved when he moved away from her. Really, for a woman who had newly found her husband in the most unusual circumstances she was remarkably calm, and he ran a bewildered hand over his dark hair, glancing back at her surreptitiously. Of course, until it was definitely proved that he was her husband she was bound to feel a little strained with him, but surely they ought to have something to say to one another. *Anything!*

'Tell me,' he said at last, 'why did you come to the clinic today? Had you heard about me? Did you suspect that I might be your husband?'

She got to her feet, tucking her hair behind her ears. 'No—no, I didn't suspect anything like that. I—I believe you know Father Juan. He visits the hospital sometimes to talk with the patients.'

'Yes, I remember him. The priest.'

'That's right. Well, he's a close friend of my aunt's, and when he dined with us the other evening, he was speaking about you. He—he said you might appreciate being able to speak with someone about England. He thought—it might jog your memory.'

'Ah, I see.' He nodded slowly. 'For a woman who has been so recently shocked, you're amazingly cool.'

She coloured. 'I'm not really. I'm a mass of nerves inside.'

He could believe that, strangely. She was nervous. But whether it was entirely because of his presence he would not have liked to say. In any event, Doctor Ramirez returned at that moment with a bottle of wine and some glasses and it was hard to tell who was the most relieved.

The celebration drink was perhaps a little premature, and he could tell from the expression in Ramirez's eyes that he was not yet wholly convinced, despite Justina's assertions, and the corresponding set of circumstances. But whichever way this turned out, it was an astounding coincidence.

Conversation became difficult and stilted, and at last Justina said she must be going. Ramirez discreetly made some excuse about having to go and see one of his patients and left them alone for a few moments before her departure, but he need not have bothered.

Now that the decision was made, Justina seemed almost eager to get away, and he made no attempt to detain her. After all, this was her problem, not his, for his involvement had to be involuntary. He wondered if she would give any sign of affection for him in her farewell, but to his surprise she shook hands with him, making some inane remark about the change of climate after England. She rode away with her escort, leaving him feeling less sure of himself than he had done before her arrival.

Later that day, he was lying on his bed, fully clothed, resting, when Sister Teresa entered his room. He opened his eyes and smiled when she approached the bed.

'What is it?' he asked. 'Come to take my pulse again?' Then he noticed the book in her hand. 'What's that you're reading?'

Sister Teresa endeavoured to assume a composed countenance. 'No, I haven't come to take your pulse, *senhor*,' she replied quietly. 'I found this book among my school textbooks, and as it's in English I thought you might like to see it.'

He sat up, swinging his feet to the floor. 'That was kind of you. What is it?'

'It is the life story of one of your British engineers—Brunel. You have heard of him?' She looked anxious.

He took the heavy volume out of her hands. Flicking over the pages, which were lavishly illustrated with Brunel's most famous achievements, he felt a stirring of interest. Isambard Kingdom Brunel. Yes, he had heard of him. A vague ache troubled his temples. Brunel. That name meant more to him than just any famous name should have done.

He looked up at Sister Teresa who was watching him nervously. 'Thank you,' he said, with a warm smile. 'I shall enjoy reading this.'

Sister Teresa bit her lip. 'You may keep it if you like, *senhor*. It is of no further use to me. Not now.'

He slid off the bed, looking down at her from his greater height. 'You're very sweet,' he murmured gently.

Sister Teresa's cheeks suffused with colour. 'Th— that's all right,' she stammered hastily, and turning she fled from the room.

He stared for several seconds at the closed door and then with a slight shrug of his broad shoulders, he sat down again on the side of the bed, looking at the book in his hands.

There was something, he didn't know what, that troubled him about this book. Somehow, somewhere, he sensed he had held the book in his hands before. But it was impossible that he should have held this particular book. He must have held another copy.

He pressed his hands to the back of his neck. Think, he commanded himself grimly, *think*!

He turned once more to the book. There was an illustration of the iron ship, the *Great Eastern*, acknowledged as Brunel's proudest achievement, and beside it on the opposite page a picture of the Clifton suspension bridge over the River Avon at Bristol. The bridge attracted his interest, and he looked thoughtfully at the slender silver span suspended from its cables above the gorge. It was a beautiful piece of engineering and he marvelled that anything so magnificent could have been built before this age of sophisticated machinery. As a boy, he had admired men like Brunel and Telford, men with image and foresight, and that was why he had wanted to be an engineer himself, why he had taken physics... science...mathematics...

He thrust the book aside with a muffled ejaculation. Dear God, was he going mad? *Engineering*! That was his career. That was what his occupation had been before the plane crash.

He got abruptly to his feet, cupping his aching head in his hands. It was all coming back now, wave after wave of painful recollection, and for a moment he thought his head would burst with the pressure.

He put out his hand to reach for the bell which would summon the attention of one of the Sisters, and then dropped it again. *No!* Not yet. Not until he was absolutely certain he wasn't imagining all this.

He sank down on to the bed again, resting his elbows on his knees, his head cradled in his hands. For a few minutes physical nausea overwhelmed him, and he had to force himself to relax completely. Maybe the effort would not have been quite so great had he not, that very day, been given an entirely different identity from which he was finding it difficult to dissociate himself, but he couldn't concentrate on that at the moment.

He knew his name. He actually knew his own name. It wasn't Andrew Douglas, or at least that wasn't what his brain told him. It was Hallam... Dominic Hallam, and he wasn't thirty-seven, he was thirty-nine. And his reasons for coming to South America were vastly different from what the girl, Justina, had said. He was an engineer. He was employed by a firm of structural and constructional engineers in London. He had been sent to Lima to design a rail link over a section of the Andes, and he had been aboard the plane to La Paz en route for Callao, Lima's international airport.

He found a stub of a cheroot in his pocket and lit it with slightly unsteady fingers. It was easy to see why his disappearance had not been reported. The London company he worked for expected him to be in Peru, while the Peruvian government department he was to work for probably imagined he was on his way and would take some time before contacting London to find out why he had not arrived.

He drew deeply on the cheroot. It was all becoming clear and things were beginning to fall into place, rather like the pieces of a jig-saw puzzle. He began to recall more personal details. He didn't have a wife; at least, not now. His recollections of marital strife marked the break-up of his marriage, and after their divorce his wife had been killed in a motor accident. He could remember it all now, the whole sordid affair, and his lips twisted cynically. He had been a boy when he married Linda, that had been his wife's name, but it had not taken him long to find out what his wife was. From the beginning their marriage had been a disaster. Linda had refused to travel with him when his work took him abroad as it so often did, and consequently they spent months apart. Yet for all that, he had expected, naïvely he supposed now, that Linda should be faithful to him. Only coming back unexpectedly from a trip to South Africa he had found her with another man, and after that he would have nothing more to do with her.

She had refused to divorce him. He provided her with a meal ticket. So Dominic had waited the necessary period and obtained a divorce without her consent, rather than drag everything through the courts. When she was killed later, he had felt nothing, which seemed to prove to him that the so-called love between a man and a woman was nothing more than a physical attachment. In any event he had no intention of ever making the same mistake again, and although he found women desirable and even necessary from time to time, he never got involved.

Getting to his feet again, he walked over to his windows, looking out on the sweep of the valley. Now that his mind was becoming less confused he was faced with other problems, most particularly the young woman who had today claimed him as her husband.

He smiled wryly. Ramirez would not be surprised that things had not turned out as she expected. He had sensed that the doctor had found the whole affair rather hard to swallow, and yet what possible motive could she have for stating something like that unless she had done so in good faith? It was unfortunate that she had no adequate proof of his similarity to her husband, and no witnesses either.

He shook his head. And then a thought struck him. The name she had given him, Andrew Douglas, was not unknown to him any more. Andrew Douglas was a well-known figure in Europe, at least. And he was a racing driver. But what struck Dominic most strongly was the realisation that contrary to Justina's assertions he did not in any way resemble the man.

Oh, they had similar characteristics if you could say that height and build and colouring were similar, but facially they were not at all alike.

He pressed his balled fist against the window frame. He had been right, anyway. There was something wrong with her story. He had sensed it even before he knew his own identity. She was lying. He didn't look like her husband at all. But why should she say he did?

He turned and rested his head back against the wall. It was too much to try and speculate upon her reasons. He was tired. The effort of remembering his identity had been too much for him. What he really needed to do was lie down for a while and rest—close his eyes, and pray that when he opened them again his memory would still be there. It was frightening, he thought with grim humour. One couldn't be sure of anything any more.

He lay down on the bed wearily. He ought to call Ramirez and tell him what had happened. He would be delighted—and relieved. It would take his most difficult patient off his hands. As soon as Dominic was strong enough to travel, he could leave for Lima and take up his assignment as expected. The delay would not cause too many problems, he didn't think. Government departments, to his knowledge, were notoriously unreliable, and a month here or there wouldn't make much difference.

He closed his eyes. It was marvellous to know who

he was at last. It seemed months since he first began plaguing his brain with unanswerable questions. But now he could answer everything, and he considered, rather wryly, that Justina had probably been responsible for ruining her own plans. Without her intervention, he might not have put so much strain on his subconscious... When he awoke, he found Doctor Ramirez standing beside his bed, looking down on him with some concern.

'Ah, *senhor*! You are all right?' he frowned. 'When Constancia brought in your evening meal she was alarmed to find you unconscious.'

'Unconscious?' Dominic sat up, putting a hand to his thumping head. 'God! What a headache!'

Ramirez clicked his fingers impatiently. 'As I thought, this affair with Justina has disturbed your metabolism. I should not have allowed her to shock you like that.'

'No—please—' Dominic swallowed hard, trying to find words to say what he had to say. 'It wasn't that at all—'

'Nevertheless, it is obvious you are not as well as I had foolishly imagined. Perhaps we have been going too fast. Perhaps your improved physical condition has blinded me to the instabilities of your mental state. I should have realised...'

Dominic opened his mouth to contradict him and then closed it again. Momentarily a picture of Justina de la Roca crossed the inner recesses of his mind, and he knew a desire to know more about her, and more about the reasons behind her astounding claim. It might be crazy, but now that he knew who he was he felt no particular urgency to take up his old life. That could wait; it had waited these few weeks. It could wait a few weeks more. And if not, there were other jobs, other companies; although he knew that Lester Cunningham, managing director of Cunningham International, the company he worked for, was a personal friend, and therefore hardly likely to fire him without good reason. And what better reason did he have for remaining here, in the valley, than that of being without his memory?

So he said nothing, merely allowing Doctor Ramirez to fuss about him like a mother hen, and wondered with amused speculation how Justina would find proof enough to satisfy the doctor.

CHAPTER FOUR

'BUT, JUSTINA, you can't do it! You simply can't do it!'

The speaker was a tall dark man, lean and attractive, dressed formally in a dinner jacket, the sash of a foreign honour across his chest. Justina had caught him on his way to an official engagement, and he was walking restlessly about the room, shaking his head exasperatedly.

'I've got to do it, Luis,' Justina exclaimed wearily. 'Can't you see that? Oh, please, say you'll help me. Only you can.'

Luis Salvador folded his arms and faced her solemnly. 'Justina, you seem to be forgetting that somewhere, someone else knows this man. Some woman may be going through agonies of anxiety wondering where he might be. How can you suggest ignoring all these possibilities for the sake of—of a whim?'

'It's hardly a whim, Luis. Try and understand. I don't want Tia Renata to worry about me any more, that's all. Oh, goodness, if there was some woman worrying over this man, why hasn't she come forward? Heavens, it's been three weeks and more since the accident. There's been plenty of time for enquiries to be made.'

Luis heaved a sigh. 'You're asking the impossible.'

'Why? What am I asking that's so dreadful? Just that you should identify this man as Andrew to Doctor Ramirez. I don't expect any public announcement, or anything like that. Is it so impossible?'

Luis shook his head helplessly. He was very fond of his young cousin, and he hated disappointing her at all. And after what she had just told him about her treatment at the hands of Andrew Douglas, the *real* Andrew Douglas, that was, he would have liked to have been able to get his hands on that gentleman himself, and the fact that he was dead made little difference to the hatred he felt towards him. If he had only suspected that Justina was not happy...

Now he said: 'Justina, I'd like to help you, but as you know, enquiries are being made by the airline into the crash, and sooner or later they're bound to discover this man's real identity.'

'I know that. But these enquiries take time. And particularly in this instance when belongings have been burnt—'

'But, Justina, what will you do if he regains his memory while he's in your aunt's house?'

Justina moved her shoulders helplessly. 'Face that—if it ever happens, I suppose,' she replied slowly.

Luis made an impatient gesture. 'And what do you hope to gain by it?'

'Breathing space.'

'And Tia Renata?'

'She'll never know the difference. Her sight is failing rapidly, and besides, she doesn't have strength to question anyone about their life history. Apart from Juana, the companion, there is no one else to convince.'

'And my uncle?'

'Father Juan? Why should he question it if he has your word that Andrew is who I say he is?'

'Exactly. *My* word. It all hinges on my word!' Luis spread his hands expressively. 'Justina, you may not believe this, but my word is considered to mean something around here. You're asking me to tell a deliberate lie for no reasonable explanation that I can see. Sooner or later Tia Renata is bound to find out that Andrew is dead!'

'Why?'

'What do you mean—why?'

'Exactly what I say. Look, Luis, you know Tia Renata is very old. Doctor Ramirez doesn't hold out much hope that she will ever recover from this last attack. Not completely. She may linger on for a while, but even Father Juan is not convinced. It's perfectly possible that she need never know the truth...'

'What are you afraid of, Justina?'

Justina tugged painfully at a strand of her hair. 'I want to live my own life, Luis. Is that so much to ask? After the past three years with Andrew I couldn't bear...' She made a helpless movement of her shoulders. 'Luis, I've told you. Manuelo says—'

'Yes, yes, I know what Manuelo says.' Luis ground his teeth together impatiently.

Justina went closer to him, looking up at him appealingly. 'Luis, please,' she murmured huskily. 'Won't you help me?'

Luis looked down into her face reluctantly. She was a disturbingly attractive young woman, and he was not immune to the pleading depths of her brown eyes, or the curved lift of her lovely mouth.

'Justina,' he said heavily, 'you don't know what you're asking.'

Justina sensed that he was weakening, and her heart pounded in anticipation. 'Are you going to help me, Luis?' she asked softly, fingering the white satin sash.

Luis's jaw tightened abruptly. 'Do not try your feminine wiles on me, Justina,' he said grimly, 'or I might begin to wonder if everything you have told me about your husband is entirely true.'

Justina's hand fell away. 'That's a rotten thing to say!'

Luis half smiled. 'I agree. But it had the desired effect, wouldn't you say?'

Justina hunched her shoulders. 'This is no time for teasing.'

Luis lifted her chin. 'I agree. All right, Justina, I'll consider it. But much against my better judgement. And what happens if this becomes public?'

'Why should it? Besides, no doubt this man would be open to any reasonable offer...'

Luis sighed. 'Very well. And now I must go. I am expected at the Embassy in fifteen minutes.'

'Oh, thank you, darling, darling Luis!' Justina hugged his arm in relief.

Luis gave her an indulgent grimace. 'Go along now. Morgana will be glad of your company this evening. Tell her I'll see you both later.'

'Yes, Luis.' Justina was demure now, but he was not deceived, and he was smiling as he went out to climb into the official car.

Justina spent the evening with his wife, Morgana. They were good friends, and as Morgana was expecting their second child in a few weeks she had been unable to accompany her husband as she normally did. Justina tried to concentrate on Morgana's conversation, but her mind was totally absorbed with what she was intending to do, and she was relieved to escape to her room at the end of the evening.

Now that Luis had overcome the most difficult obstacle for her, she had time to consider the dangers of creating such an alliance. In other circumstances, she would have baulked at becoming involved with any man, and particularly one who was as physically disturbing as the stranger in the clinic.

Since her marriage to Andrew her natural instincts had been dulled, and she felt she could not bear the thought of any man being that close to her ever again.

And recalling that moment in Doctor Ramirez's office when the man had attempted to touch her hair, she shivered violently. What would she do if he tried to enforce the rights he thought he had? Could her strength of will carry her that far? Could she actually go through with such a relationship even knowing what was involved?

She rolled about restlessly in the silken sheeted bed in her room at the Palacio. Until now, she had been intent upon getting Luis to agree to her appeals. But now that he had, now that success was within her grasp, she felt afraid.

There were so many pitfalls to encounter, so many obstacles that could raise their ugly heads. Was she capable of conveying to this man that their relationship should remain on a platonic basis until his memory returned? Would he agree to such an arrangement? And if not, what could she do? If once she claimed this man as her husband, if once she removed him from the comparative security of the hospital, would she be able to control him?

She sat up in the bed burying her face in her hands. Was anything worth all this heart-searching? She paused a moment to wonder why Tia Renata should be so concerned about her future? Why couldn't she leave her to make her own way, as she, Renata, had done? For now she was caught between the devil and the deep blue sea. On the one hand, she wanted her aunt to recover, wanted desperately to see her well again; and on the other she knew how much simpler things would be if her aunt were no longer around to ask questions she could not answer.

The following day, Luis flew with her back to the valley. They used the presidential plane to reach Voltio, and flew on from there by helicopter.

It was a glorious day, and Justina tried to pretend that she was young again, and that she and Luis were not bent on a mission which could have disastrous consequences for her. If Luis was conscious of her trepidation, he made no mention of the fact, and she wondered rather uncharitably whether he thought that whatever happened it was on her own head.

They landed on a dusty plateau high above the valley, and were driven down to the clinic in a battered Landrover. Luis, dressed in jeans and an open-necked shirt, looked vastly different from the formally attired *presidente* of the night before, and Justina thought how easy it was to see why the people accepted him when he could adapt himself so smoothly into their ways.

Doctor Ramirez was in his office when they arrived and he greeted Luis warmly. 'How good to see you again, my friend,' he exclaimed, shaking his hand. 'And how is Morgana?'

Luis smiled. 'Morgana, as you know, is blooming,' he remarked humorously. 'But impatient, of course.'

'Of course.' Ramirez smiled. Then he looked at

Justina. 'And you, Justina? You are here to have Luis meet your husband?'

Justina coloured. Ramirez could disconcert her by his intent appraisal. 'That's right,' she agreed shortly. 'Er—where is—Andrew?'

Ramirez frowned. 'He is in his room.' He looked at Luis. 'Tell me, Luis: do you not find this story of Justina's hard to take?'

Luis hesitated. 'Not particularly,' he said at last, when Justina's nerves were beginning to fray. 'After all, it seems the most logical explanation.'

'But was this man's name on the flight schedule?'

Luis hesitated. 'As far as I am aware, from what I have learned from the airline company in Rio, the schedules were drawn up several days before take-off. Several passengers' names were later withdrawn owing to cancellations, and others inserted. No one seems entirely knowledgeable about how many passengers were on this flight.'

Justina sought Luis's hand and squeezed it gratefully, but he detached himself, as Ramirez went on:

'But surely this is a shocking state of affairs. How do airlines continue to function so inefficiently?'

'Had there not been an accident, there would have been records on board the aircraft,' replied Luis smoothly. 'No doubt there will be an enquiry in due course. Now, do you suppose we could see—this man? I have to be back in Queranova by late this afternoon. There is a meeting I must attend.'

'Of course.' Doctor Ramirez was diverted and Justina breathed a sigh of relief. So far, so good.

When Ramirez opened the door of his patient's room, the man was lounging lazily in a chair by the window reading a heavy book which he put aside immediately at their entrance. He rose to his feet and faced them curiously, his eyes flickering almost insolently over Justina. A feeling of indignation swept over her in that moment. He was bigger than she remembered, as tall as Luis, and more muscularly built, and there was a half mocking gleam in his grey eyes which she felt sure had not been there before.

Luis, with an amazing amount of self-confidence, she thought, strode forward at once, grasping the man by the hand and staring into his face disbelievingly.

'Andrew!' he exclaimed, in an astounded tone. '*Deus*, it is you! I couldn't believe it when Justina told me you were here!'

Dominic was incredulous, and for a moment he could only stare at the tall stranger in amazement. *Holy cow*, he thought bewilderedly. *Was everyone out of their minds around here*?

'Am—am I supposed to know you?' he enquired faintly.

Justina moved forward now. 'This is Luis, Andrew,' she said carefully. 'My cousin Luis.'

Dominic frowned. He had heard that name before...*Luis*! Of course, the last time she was here Ramirez had mentioned his name. He was the *presidente* of this small country. The man who was reputed to have introduced them.

'Ah, yes,' he said now. The whole affair intrigued him more by the minute and he couldn't wait to hear what they would say next. One way or the other Justina was determined to prove to Ramirez that he was her husband, and somehow she had enlisted the aid of her cousin, the *presidente*. 'I—aren't you supposed to have introduced Justina and myself?'

Luis inclined his head. 'That is correct. At the reception in Queranova.'

Dominic nodded, glancing towards Ramirez. Then he looked back at the *presidente*. 'And you're here to attempt to confirm my identity, is that it?'

'Of course.' Luis released his hand and regarded him intently. 'I am beginning to believe my cousin was right in her assumption. You are certain you can remember none of this?'

Dominic half smiled, and then controlled his features. Of course this man, this Luis, would need to feel pretty certain that he did not remember anything.

'I'm afraid I'm completely in the dark,' he lied smoothly. 'As you can imagine, if my wife's image means nothing to me, how could yours do otherwise?'

'Indeed.' Luis seemed inclined to accept this view. He turned to Ramirez and shrugged. 'As far as I can see, there is little doubt that this man is who Justina says he is. Naturally, in matters of this sort, time alone will solve the problem for us, will it not, Antonio?'

Ramirez sighed. 'You are probably right. There is absolutely no reason why—why Senhor Douglas should not recover his memory completely. But when that will be...' He spread his hands helplessly.

Luis turned to Justina. 'So what do you want to do? I suggest you remove—Andrew from the clinic forthwith. Perhaps in other surroundings his memory may reassert itself. We will see. In any event, Antonio, I do not see any reason for this matter to be made public knowledge. As my cousin was expecting her husband...'

'Of course, Luis. I understand.' Ramirez nodded.

'So now—' Luis turned back to Dominic. 'I understand all your belongings were destroyed in the fire. If you can give me your measurements I will have my tailor forward some clothes to the *castelo* ready for your arrival.'

Dominic frowned. '*Castelo?*...'

It was not difficult feigning ignorance in these matters. After all, he knew nothing of Justina and her affairs and that was the truth.

'The *castelo* is—*was* my home before our marriage,' Justina was explaining now. She managed a forced smile. 'I can see I shall have to give you a complete run-down on our personal affairs.'

'That you will.' Dominic allowed his eyes to wander lazily across her face and was amused to see the hot colour surge into her cheeks. Really, for a woman who had been married, (at least he supposed she really had been married to this Andrew Douglas) she seemed incredibly naïve; but don't let that fool you, he told himself grimly. Anyone who could perpetrate such an arrangement without knowing the slightest thing about their involuntary assistant was no innocent. Whatever this elaborate charade was all about, he felt an intense feeling of contempt for her unscrupulous behaviour.

Now Luis turned to the door. 'Well, Justina, I must be going. I promised Morgana I would not be too long.'

'Of course.' Justina moved towards the door, too, but Ramirez stopped her with a casual movement of his hand.

'I will see your cousin off, Justina,' he said smilingly. 'I will have Guido bring the Landrover back after he has taken Luis up to the plateau, and he can run you home then. It will give you some little time with—your husband.'

Dominic wondered how Justina would react to this arrangement and was gratified to see her disconcertment. But short of appearing indifferent there was nothing she could do, and he watched cynically as Luis kissed her gently on both cheeks before taking his departure.

After the door had closed behind them, she moved jerkily about the room, and he wondered what she would do if he touched her. She knew he wasn't her husband just as well as he did, but his was the stronger position. She didn't know that he knew anything.

And that being so, he thought coolly, why shouldn't he play a few games with her?

She was standing by the window, staring out on the sunlit mountainside, her expression withdrawn, her thoughts obviously far from this small, cell-like room.

He went up to her, standing just behind her, and he could smell the fragrant scent of the perfume she was wearing. Today she was dressed in a slim-fitting smock and navy trousers, and with her hair loose about her shoulders, she looked disturbingly feminine. And he was only human, after all.

He put his hands on her shoulders and she started as before, only this time his fingers tightened, gripping the narrow bones almost cruelly. 'Justina!' He said her name softly, and he could feel her trembling body beneath his hands. 'Justina, don't you think it's time we renewed other things besides identities?'

She dragged herself away from him, a hand pressed to her throat, her eyes wild and apprehensive. 'Please, don't! Don't touch me!' she said chokingly.

'Why?' He put his hands on his hips, standing before her, big and powerful in his masculinity. 'Why mustn't I touch you, Justina? You are my wife, after all.'

'I—I know that.' She shook her head helplessly. 'I—I was afraid of this. I was—afraid you would have forgotten.'

'Forgotten? Forgotten what?'

Justina made a concerted effort to gather her composure. 'I—I've been ill. My—my nerves!' She seemed to shake herself. 'I—I can't stand anyone to—to touch me!'

'*God!*' He raked a hand through his hair. 'You don't actually expect me to believe that, do you?'

'Why not?' Justina was shivering as she thrust back the heavy weight of her hair. 'It—it's the truth.'

'Oh, is it?' He tugged absently at the laces of his shirt, loosening it so that she could see the thick growth of hair that darkened his chest. 'And what caused—this condition?'

She drew a trembling breath. 'I—I don't know. Your—your racing, perhaps. I—I was always nervous when you were on the track.'

'I see.' He narrowed his eyes. 'And I suppose you've had medical treatment. I suppose Doctor Ramirez knows of this—condition.'

'*No!*' She pressed her lips together helplessly. 'Oh, please, don't let's have an argument over it. Just give me time—that's all I ask.'

'Do I take it there is no medical condition, then?'

'You can take it whatever way you like.' She heaved a sigh. 'Andrew, be reasonable! We—we aren't even certain you are who I think you are.'

'You were certain enough a few days ago.'

'Well, we shall have to see, shan't we?'

He tilted his head. 'And what more natural way—'

'No!' She reached for her handbag and extracted a packet of cigarettes. 'Do you—I mean—will you have one?'

'Do I smoke these?' He took one from her.

'No. You smoke an American brand. I prefer something milder.'

He inclined his head and while she sought about in her bag for her lighter he produced a box of matches and lit both their cigarettes coolly and deliberately.

'Thank you.' She puffed rather nervously at hers, causing herself to choke and then cough ignominiously.

'Won't you sit down?' He indicated the bed, but she chose the hard chair by the window where he had been sitting on their arrival. He seated himself on the bed, one knee drawn up, his chin resting upon it, and regarded her intently. 'Tell me,' he said. 'What makes a beautiful woman like you afraid of her husband?'

'I'm not afraid,' she denied hotly. 'But you must realise that it's difficult for me to get used to someone who doesn't even remember my name.'

'It's difficult for me, too,' he reminded her dryly.

'It's different for a man,' she retorted quickly.

'Why is it?'

She flushed again. 'Stop making me put everything

into words of one syllable! You can't have forgotten that!'

He smiled mockingly. 'Aren't you afraid that my new-found independence may go to my head?'

'What do you mean?' She frowned.

'I mean that as I don't remember you or anything about you, I might find diversion—elsewhere.'

She stared at him impotently. 'You mean if I don't allow—that is, if I refuse to—oh, you know what I mean!'

'That's right.'

'You're being deliberately provocative!' she accused him angrily. 'Let's at least try and behave like civilised human beings! Now...' She endeavoured to bring the conversation into less personal channels. 'I suggest I tell you a little about the situation at my aunt's house.'

He listened in silence, watching the expressive features of her face. He was interested, or perhaps intrigued was a better description, and he absorbed what she told him without difficulty. He supposed he was in a similar position to that of a spy. He was assuming a new identity, and he had no way of knowing where that identity might lead him.

CHAPTER FIVE

JUSTINA DRESSED for dinner with care, trying to still the trembling sensation which had invaded her lower limbs, and which refused to be displaced. Everything was going smoothly, so why was she so nervous? What possible reason could she have for feeling so apprehensive?

She seated herself in front of her dressing table, beginning to brush her hair with long rhythmic strokes. This was one occupation which usually calmed her, but tonight even it did not have the desired effect.

And of course, if she was truthful with herself, she could put her finger on the whole cause of her anxiety. In the next bedroom, only a locked door away from her own suite of rooms, the man she had claimed as being Andrew Douglas, her husband, was bathing and changing for dinner, too.

She heaved a sigh and studied her reflection in the dressing table mirror. It had all been so easy, incredibly so. With Luis's backing, her aunt's companion could do nothing but accept that this man was indeed her husband, and as she had never met him before that presented no difficulties.

Her aunt had been informed this afternoon, but then she had been told only part of the truth. Her information was that Andrew had newly arrived in Monteraverde, and she had been placated. She had not yet met him, of course, that would come later, but Justina could see no problems there. So far as Tia Renata was concerned, Andrew's arrival had stilled her suspicions and she was content.

But Justina was anything but content. She was beginning to appreciate the difficulties involved when one attempted to use someone else to one's own advantage. One tended to forget that a human being was not a machine; that it had feelings and failings, and the man she had chosen as her accessory seemed deliberately intent on being as difficult as possible.

Or maybe that was her imagination. After all, he believed her to be his wife. Why else would she have taken him into her home, provided him with food and clothing? And again, it was unnatural for her to expect him to behave in exactly the way she would have chosen. He had a mind of his own and she must endeavour to give him no grounds for imagining that everything was not as it should be.

But it was terribly difficult for her to behave naturally with him. Apart from the obvious obstacles to their relationship, she found images of Andrew's maliciousness continually intruding upon her mind in his presence, and she still flinched, inwardly at least, whenever he came near her.

However, she firmly believed that sooner or later he would grow tired of baiting her, and then perhaps she would have some peace. Until then, she was committed to hiding her squeamishness in his presence.

It wasn't that he was not an attractive man. On the contrary, she could well believe that plenty of women would fall over themselves to be in her position. But during her life with Andrew she had met lots of attractive men, and in her experience they were all alike. They had little or no respect for her sex, and their sole occupation was concerned with finding ways of manoeuvring their unwilling victims into complete submission. She ought to know. Andrew had been a master of the art, and in the beginning, when she had still believed he was a man of substance, she had wondered why he had ever troubled to marry her at all. Indeed, during the course of their unhappy association, she had wished many times that she had not been the innocent she had been before marriage, and that she had had an affair with Andrew. If she had known before what she so brutally learned afterwards she would never have gone through with it.

But Andrew had been clever. He had known how precarious the situation was, and he had taken no risks before the wedding. Even Tia Renata had been taken in by him.

Now she rose from the stool on which she had been sitting, satisfied that her make-up was satisfactory.

She wore few cosmetics, relying mainly on eye-shadow and a colourless lustre for her mouth.

She lifted the gown she was to wear that evening and stepped into it. Long and white, it accentuated her almost virginal beauty, and she hoped it would have the effect of keeping her adopted husband at a distance. Her hair was loose, as usual, and it shone from the brushing she had given it, while long diamond earrings swung glintingly in and out of its dull-gold thickness.

Taking a deep breath, she walked determinedly towards the door and as she did so she heard a knock on the communicating door between her room and the one next door. The handle turned, refused to give, and then was shaken impatiently.

'Justina!' His voice was abrupt. 'Open this door, Justina!'

She hesitated, wondering whether she should pretend to have left the bedroom, but then decided that he was quite capable of walking out of his room and along the corridor to hers to find out for himself. Pressing her lips together in irritation, she moved across to the communicating door, and turned the key in the lock.

Immediately the door gave inwards, and she had to step back to avoid being knocked over. Straightening her shoulders, she gave him what she hoped was a composed stare, but he seemed indifferent to her attitudes. In the dinner suit Luis had had sent on for him, he looked bigger and broader and more attractive than ever, and it crossed her mind that perhaps she had been foolhardy in imagining she could control such a man. If she had had a choice, she would have chosen someone entirely different: smaller for one thing, and polite and biddable, not this arrogant male who was confronting her with indignant annoyance.

'We don't lock doors between man and wife in England, Justina,' he said, his thick lashes veiling the expression in eyes which she sensed were a cold grey at this moment. 'My memory does not desert me on matters of that sort.'

She moved awkwardly, irritated anew at being put at a disadvantage, and then said: 'I'm sorry. That door has been locked for some considerable time. It never occurred to me to try it.'

Scepticism marred his lean features. 'Is that so?'

'Yes, it is so.' She adopted a cold hauteur. 'Are you calling me a liar?'

He shook his head slowly. 'Leave it. You're looking particularly beautiful this evening. I am allowed to admire you, aren't I? If only from a distance.'

'Don't be objectionable!' she snapped shortly, stung by the sarcasm in his voice. 'Look, this is our first evening—together. Can't we at least try and behave naturally...'

'That's what I'm trying to do,' he remarked mockingly.

'Oh, you're impossible!' She walked quickly across

the bedroom, lifting her evening bag on the way. 'I'm going to see Tia Renata. Do you want to come?'

'If you like.' He was indifferent. He looked round her bedroom with interest, his eyes flickering over the assortment of jars and bottles on her dressing table, the drift of pink negligée which was strewn carelessly across the foot of the satin quilted bed. His expression hardened slightly. 'Don't tell me any man has ever shared this room.'

Justina tightened her lips. 'No—man has.' She swallowed with difficulty, her throat dry. 'I told you. We—we lived in England.'

'And where was our home?'

'London.' She was abrupt.

'Indeed.' He regarded her musingly. 'And I suppose we'll be going back there soon.'

'*No*! That is—not until my aunt's better.'

'But how can I neglect my affairs for so long?' he persisted. 'Oughtn't I to be attending to business matters—'

'I've told you, you're a racing driver. You have no—business matters to attend to.'

'Then surely there are races I'm expected to enter—'

'Oh, *come a breca*!' she cried tremulously. 'Will you stop asking so many questions?' She wrenched open the bedroom door and stepped out into the corridor.

His eyes narrowed. 'I'm sorry. I was just trying to piece my life together.'

Justina was full of remorse. 'I'm sorry, too,' she exclaimed, with a sigh, watching him follow her out of the room and close the door. 'I—I'm on edge; my nerves…'

'Ah, yes, your nerves.' He regarded her enigmatically, and with a muffled ejaculation she turned and walked away along the corridor, uncaring if he followed her.

Renata de la Roca was waiting for them. Justina had promised to come back later bringing her husband, and now that the moment had arrived it was nerve-racking. Justina found she was trembling as she pushed open her aunt's door and entered the stuffy, enclosed atmosphere of her aunt's apartment.

He was behind her, however, and as she approached the bed he came to stand beside her, looking down compassionately at the frail form of the old lady. Renata's puzzled frown of awareness gave way to a smile of recognition as Nurse Gomez told her who was here, and then the nurse drew back to allow Justina to take her aunt's hand.

'Hello, *amada*,' she said gently. 'How are you?'

Renata held her fingers quite tightly for a moment, and then she held out her hand towards Justina's companion. 'Andrew?' she murmured questioningly. 'Andrew, are you there?'

'Yes, I'm here, Tia Renata,' he said firmly, taking

her hand into his strong brown one. 'It's good—to see you again.'

Renata frowned. 'We were anxious about you, weren't we, Justina? You have been so long in coming. And I wanted to see you.'

'Well, I'm here now, Tia Renata. And—you can see me.'

Renata shook her head slowly, frowning. 'Unfortunately, my sight is not what it was. But I can touch you, and hear you, and feel your flesh against mine. Why have you not come back to see me all these years? Keeping Justina away from me in England. You know she has not been happy.'

Justina felt the hot colour surge into her cheeks and was conscious of his fleeting speculative gaze upon her.

'Hasn't she?' he was saying now. 'I didn't know that.'

'Of course you did.' Renata's voice could become surprisingly strong when there was something she wanted to convey. 'All this mad dashing about the world. It's not good for a woman. A woman needs a settled home and a family. When are you and Justina going to have a family, Andrew?'

He glanced again at Justina, shrugging his shoulders mockingly, so that she pressed her lips together and refused to look at him. She was beginning to wish she had not brought him to see Tia Renata this evening.

'Soon,' he said now. 'These things take time, Tia Renata.'

Tia Renata clicked her tongue. 'Not so much time, Andrew. You're a man, aren't you? I wouldn't have thought you would have found the task so difficult.'

He half smiled to himself, and Justina hated him in that moment. It didn't matter to her then that she was the instigator of all this. All she could think was that he was an impostor, and he was deliberately holding her up to ridicule. She was tempted to denounce him there and then and to hell with the consequences, but the moment passed and she seethed in silence.

'Justina hasn't felt well enough to consider such a possibility,' he went on annoyingly.

Renata frowned again. 'Hasn't felt well enough? Justina, is this true? Have you had some illness which you've kept from me?'

Justina cast a venomous glance in his direction. 'Of course not, Tia Renata. I—I've just had—a little trouble with my nerves, that's all.'

'But you never told me. Does Ramirez know? Is he treating you?'

'*Deus*, it's not as serious as all that,' she cried. 'Andrew—shouldn't have mentioned it.'

'Why not?' His eyes were mocking. 'Better that than have your aunt imagine we don't intend to have children.'

Justina clenched her fists. He was so cool, so

amused, so adept at taking a rise out of her. She was furious.

'I think we should be going,' she said now. 'We don't want to tire Tia Renata.'

'I'm not tired,' protested the old lady, but Nurse Gomez came forward at once.

'Your niece is right, *senhora*,' she said firmly. 'You have had enough excitement for one day.'

'Oh, very well.' Renata was reluctant to release his hand. She looked up at the blur of his face, and said urgently: 'You will come and see me again, Andrew, won't you?'

He smiled down on her, touching her lined cheek with a gentle finger. 'Of course, if you want me to. I'm at your disposal. Just say the word.'

'Come along, Andrew.' Justina's tone was chilling, but he seemed unperturbed, and it was he whom Tia Renata urged again to return.

Outside, Justina left him to descend the twisting staircase in frozen silence, and not until they reached the lounge and encountered Juana did she endeavour to appear conciliatory, offering him a drink and allowing him the task of preparing one for her, too.

Juana regarded him with interest, putting her sewing aside, and smiling on his easy familiarity. Justina continued to feel her temper simmering. What was wrong with everybody? Why did they persist in regarding this man they assumed to be her husband so sympathetically, so responsively? What was there about him that instilled them with this feeling of generosity? Her aunt was rarely so talkative with strangers, and after all, that was what he was, be he Andrew Douglas or not.

The evening meal passed without incident and afterwards they all adjourned to the lounge for coffee. Justina was still edgy, but her adopted husband seemed to have no such problems. He wandered round until he unearthed an old radiogram in a corner, and spent the remainder of the evening playing some of the ancient records he found in the cupboard beneath.

Juana retired to bed around ten o'clock, and Justina, who had been flicking disinterestedly through some magazines, asked him whether he would like another drink.

'Alcohol, do you mean?' he enquired lazily. He was lounging in a chair beside the radiogram, one leg resting by the ankle across the knee of the other.

'No. Actually I meant—tea, or something. Andrew always liked tea—that is—*you* always liked tea last thing at night.'

His eyes flickered and she cursed herself for her carelessness. 'Did I?' he commented. 'I wouldn't know. But okay—if you want some, we'll have it.'

'*I* don't want it,' she retorted impatiently. 'I just thought you might—seeing that—that you used to like it.'

'Yes.' He lowered his leg to the floor, and stretched lazily. 'Well, to be quite honest, I'm ready for bed.'

'Oh, of course! I'm sorry!' Justina was contrite. She had forgotten he was so newly recovered from his injuries. 'I—I'm afraid, I never thought.'

'That's all right. I'm not an invalid, you know. I just get tired easily at this stage.'

Justina ran her tongue over her dry lips. 'Well, you go on up, then,' she said. 'I—I'll just tidy up down here and tell Benita we shan't need anything else.'

He hesitated. 'All right.' He moved towards the door. 'I'll see you later, then.'

Justina coloured. 'Oh—well—no, I don't think so. I mean—well, it's too early—'

His expression hardened. 'I'm not suggesting we're about to sleep together,' he remarked harshly. 'But as our rooms adjoin, I naturally assumed we'd say good-night there.'

Justina plucked nervously at the sleeve of her gown. 'Very well.'

His gaze flickered over her appraisingly for a moment and then he turned and walked out of the room.

After he had gone she heaved a shaking breath. Oh, God, she thought weakly, what a moment that had been!

When she went upstairs, the door between their two rooms was closed and she regarded it doubtfully. He must have closed it. It had been open when she went downstairs for dinner.

Normally she undressed in her bedroom, but to-night she gathered up her nightgown and dressing gown and went into her bathroom, locking the door securely behind her. Only then did she feel safe.

When she emerged however, her room was as before and she clicked her tongue in exasperation. What should she do? If she went to open the adjoining door it would look as though she was willing to enter into a closer association with him, and that was the very last thing she wanted to achieve. Perhaps he was asleep. Perhaps he had closed the door while he got undressed and forgotten to open it again. If he wanted the door open, he could open it himself.

On impulse she tiptoed across the room and listened at the door. There was no sound from the room beyond and she sighed. He must be asleep, she decided at last. Recalling his belligerence earlier in the evening, she couldn't believe there could be any other solution.

She walked back to her bed. The covers had been turned down by the maid in her absence and the peach-coloured sheets looked cool and inviting. She took off her negligée and slid into the bed, tugging the cord that put out the lamps.

In the darkness, she could see a line of light along the bottom of the adjoining door. He had either fallen asleep with the light on, or he was still awake. She sighed again, in the darkness. Everything had seemed so simple when she had considered all this, and now suddenly everything seemed immensely complex.

She rolled on to her stomach, determinedly punching her pillow into shape. It was no good worrying now. She was committed and for better or worse there was nothing she could do about it.

But sleep was elusive. Her mind was too active, and she was intensely conscious of him in the next room. What if he decided to assert his rights? What if he suddenly opened that door and marched in here and demanded her submission? What could she do? Could she call for help, and if so, who would help her? He was her husband; no one here knew otherwise. And he had every right to sleep with his wife if he felt so inclined. As it was, Benita had seemed surprised when Justina had insisted that they had *adjoining* suites, rather than a joint one. And Tia Renata would not be too pleased either if ever she found out.

But she wouldn't, Justina assured herself firmly. She was confined to her room and had no earthly reason to question the sleeping arrangements of her niece and her husband.

But what if she did? a small voice plagued her. What if she asked the man she thought was Andrew about Justina's attitude to that kind of relationship? Tia Renata could be infuriatingly personal if the mood took her, and knowing what she did about this man, Justina felt sure he would delight in informing her reproachfully that his wife wouldn't allow him near her.

She rolled on to her back again, biting her lips. The line of light beneath the adjoining door had gone. He had turned out his light. Was he now asleep? She shivered, even though it was quite a warm night. He probably was one of those people who fell asleep the minute their heads touched the pillow.

Justina fumed. Here she was, lying here, at the mercy of her wild speculations, while he was most probably comfortably relaxed next door, content in his new-found identity.

CHAPTER SIX

DURING THE NEXT few days, things seemed to settle down at the *castelo*.

Justina found that Andrew—she had no other means of identifying him—was intensely interested in his surroundings, and because of this she was able to arrange outings for him into the majestic countryside flanking the *castelo*.

Anton, the boy who had accompanied her on her trip to the mission hospital, was always available, and as Andrew had proved to be an adept horseman that presented no problems. Travelling on horseback was by far the most satisfactory means of transport, for some of the tracks were too narrow to take even the Landrover.

In the beginning, he had expected her to accompany them, but Justina had so far succeeded in avoiding this. She had made various excuses ranging from her aunt's precarious state of health to her own physical condition, but she was aware that while Andrew seemed to accept her excuses the expression in his eyes revealed his scepticism.

No further mention had been made of their sleeping arrangements, and although Justina was relieved, she couldn't help but feel apprehensive. He was simply not the kind of man to enable one to take anything for granted, and sometimes she wished he had had a row about it and brought it out into the open. This silent game of cat and mouse was disastrous to her nervous system.

By now, he knew almost everything he needed to know about his assumed background, and occasionally she paused to wonder whether this new identity would in any way retard his natural progress towards recovery. At times like these she realised how impulsively she had taken over this man's life, and how little thought she had given to the fact that he had a mind of his own. She did not care to speculate too long on the consequences of what might happen if he should discover his true identity, deciding that when that day came she would face it then. After all, the fact that no one had so far come forward to identify him pointed to his lack of background, and she could only assume he was the kind of man you sometimes found in out-of-the-way places, making his living as best he could. His circumstances seemed to be ideal for her purposes and had he been less of an enigma, she could have felt almost content at the way things were working out.

She regretted deceiving her aunt, of course, but maybe she could be forgiven as her aunt was so ill. No matter what the outcome, the realisation that her niece was now a widow was bound to be a shock. And she was being spared that.

Justina started suddenly as Juana entered the small study where she was sitting checking her aunt's accounts. The older woman had a habit of moving silently about the *castelo* and Justina resented her assumption that she could treat her in the same way as she had used to treat Renata.

'There is a young woman waiting to speak with you, *senhora*,' she intoned politely.

Justina frowned. 'A young woman? Who?'

'A Senhorita Garcia, *senhora*. She says she is an old friend of yours.'

'Senhorita Garcia—*Amalia Garcia*!' Justina was stunned. She had attended school with Amalia Garcia, but it was some years since her family had moved to the United States and consequently they had lost touch with one another.

'I think that was the name, *senhora*,' Juana was aloof. 'Do you wish me to show her in here?' Her tone intimated that she was not the parlourmaid.

Justina shook her head hastily, and slid off her chair. 'Of course not, Juana. I'll come.'

Amalia Garcia awaited her in the hall of the *castelo*. She was looking about her casually as Justina approached and Justina had ample opportunity to observe that Amalia had matured into a most attractive young woman. Excessively dark hair was bound round her head in a coronet of braids and a slim-fitting suit of pink linen accentuated her slender figure. She was perhaps not so tall as Justina, but she carried herself with elegance, and when she turned and saw her friend a warm smile enveloped her features.

Justina ran to her with an exclamation of pleasure. 'Amalia, it is you! Good heavens, what are you doing here?'

Amalia returned Justina's hug of welcome rather less enthusiastically, detaching herself to run a hand over her sleek head of hair. 'Am I not allowed to come here, then?' she countered charmingly.

Justina shook her head and sighed. 'It's just such an unexpected surprise. I thought you were still in the States.'

'I was, darling. I do live there, you know. But my father had business in Rio, and I suggested I came south with him and spent several days with my aunt.' Justina remembered that Amalia's mother had a sister who still lived in the valley.

'I see.' Justina nodded.

'And when Tia Isabela told me that you were here, staying with your aunt, too, it was too good an opportunity to miss.'

Justina nodded again. 'Well, do come in. We have so much to talk about.' She glanced round and found Juana standing watching them. Biting her lip in impatience, she said: 'Do you think you could ask Benita if we could have some coffee, Juana?'

The elderly companion straightened her shoulders and for a moment Justina thought she was about to refuse, but then she nodded and walked slowly away.

'Who is that?' whispered Amalia, conspiratorially, as they entered the lounge. 'Quite a frightening old thing, isn't she?'

'Juana? Frightening?' Justina shrugged. 'I wouldn't say that. But she does tend to—well, eavesdrop.' Then she drew Amalia down on to the couch. 'But never mind about her, tell me about yourself. What have you been doing in the States? You're not married?'

'No, darling. But you are, I hear.'

Justina coloured. 'Well, yes.'

'You don't sound exactly enthusiastic, darling.' Amalia's brows quirked teasingly.

'It's not that.' Justina was hasty. 'I—I want to hear about what you've been doing. I expect it's all been very exciting.'

Amalia made a moue with her lips. 'Some,' she agreed indifferently. 'Where we live, in California, we have marvellous weather, and one can swim all the year round. But I suppose I'm a Monteraverdian at heart, and I prefer it here, in the valley.'

Justina smiled reminiscently. 'Yes, so do I,' she agreed warmly.

Amalia shrugged. 'I'd get bored here, of course. At least, in the States one has a constant round of entertainment. There are parties and beach barbecues; that sort of thing. And shows and films and exhibitions. I've become quite an expert on modern art.'

Justina listened with interest, but no feeling of envy. This was the kind of life Andrew had enjoyed, constantly requiring some new stimulus to whet his appetites. Amalia should have married Andrew. Maybe she could have stood up to it rather better than she, Justina, had.

'But what about you?' Amalia was saying now. 'My aunt tells me your husband is here at the *castelo* with you. Will I be able to meet him? I'm sure you've had a far more exciting time than I've had.'

Justina's nails closed on the palms of her hands. This was a situation she had not prepared herself for. Amalia was from the United States. It was possible that she had heard of Andrew Douglas; even seen pictures of him! Then she forced herself to be calm. It was possible, yes, but highly improbable. To begin with, Andrew had not been a world-famous name, and his racing had been confined to the European circuits. And besides, racing drivers were seldom photographed unless they were constantly winning races, and Andrew had seldom done that. She was worrying unnecessarily, and she managed to force a smile to her lips and answer Amalia.

'Of course you'll be able to meet Andrew,' she said. 'Perhaps not today, but some other time. He's out at the moment.'

Amalia looked disappointed. 'Oh, that's a pity!

Still, never mind. I'm sure there'll be lots of opportunities while I'm here. Now that we've met up again,
I'm hoping we can keep in touch.'

'Yes.' Justina was doubtful, but she was saved
from making any further comment by the arrival of
Benita with the tray of coffee and biscuits that Juana
had ordered. The elderly companion had not returned
and yet Justina had the feeling that she would not be
far away.

Over coffee, Amalia questioned her about her aunt.
She knew Renata de la Roca only slightly, but she
was concerned to hear of the seriousness of her illness.

'And how long do you and your husband intend to
stay?' she asked, helping herself to another biscuit.

Justina shrugged. 'I don't know. I—well, for some
time, I should think. Doctor Ramirez is not hopeful
that my aunt will ever make a full recovery, and I
couldn't go and leave her.'

'No, I can understand that,' Amalia nodded. 'And
your husband has nothing to make him return to Europe?'

Justina flushed. 'Well, he—he doesn't have a regular job, you see. His—his father left him comfortably—off.' Her nerves tightened at the deliberate lie.
If only Tia Renata had known what a fallacy that
statement had been. But somehow that had been one
thing Justina had never found herself able to tell her
aunt in her letters.

'Oh, I see.' Amalia was interested. 'That's very lucky, isn't it? I mean—had your husband had to return to England, no doubt you would have wanted to go with him. He is English, isn't he? Tia Isabela said as much.'

'Yes.' Justina's voice was scarcely audible, and looking down she caught sight of her wrist watch. It was almost twelve; almost lunch time, in fact. Would Andrew be back for lunch? Her heart sank. She was not looking forward to the prospect of introducing him to Amalia. Not today, anyway, not yet... She had fondly imagined they could stay here without ever meeting anyone. Her aunt's life was so remote. She had foolishly thought theirs would be the same.

But her innate good manners would not allow her to ignore her most obvious course of action, so she said with a smile: 'You'll stay to lunch, of course, Amalia?'

Amalia glanced at her narrow cocktail watch. 'Goodness, is it that time already?' She rose abruptly to her feet and Justina got up also. 'No, thank you, darling, I'm afraid I can't. My aunt is expecting me back. We're having guests to lunch, and I promised I'd only be an hour.'

Justina was inordinately relieved, but she expressed suitable regret and they moved towards the door of the lounge. 'You must come again,' she said firmly.

Amalia touched her cheek. 'Oh, I will, darling. But actually, you might come to us first. Tia Isabela is having some people to dinner tomorrow evening. Just a few friends; people you may know, too. Why don't you and your husband join us?'

Justina opened her mouth to make some polite refusal, when they heard the sound of the heavy hall door opening and men's voices. Amalia glanced at Justina in anticipation, giving her a teasing smile, and presently heavy booted treads crossed the polished wooden floor. The man halted abruptly in the entrance to the lounge looking first at Justina and then more thoroughly at Amalia.

In riding breeches and boots, a thick cream sweater with a roll collar accentuating his dark masculinity, he looked big and disturbingly attractive, and Justina felt her heart flutter a little as she noticed the intent appraisal he was giving the other girl.

'Oh—oh, hello, Andrew,' she said, speaking English now. 'How—how fortunate you've arrived back in time to meet—an old friend.'

'Of yours or mine?' he queried mockingly, and Amalia's laugh echoed about the tapestry-hung apartment.

'Of mine, of course,' exclaimed Justina reprovingly, giving him a fierce stare which he chose to ignore. 'Amalia, you'll have gathered that this—this is Andrew Douglas, my—my husband.'

Amalia allowed him to take her hand, looking up at him through her lashes rather alluringly. 'Hello, Andrew,' she said huskily.

'Hello, Amalia.' Andrew held her hand rather longer than was necessary, and then allowed her to withdraw her fingers. 'I wouldn't have gone out if I'd known we were to have such a charming guest.'

Justina pressed her lips together. 'I didn't know Amalia was coming,' she denied sharply. 'The last time Amalia and I saw one another was four years ago.'

'Really?' Andrew moved into the room, reaching familiarly for a cheroot from the carved box on a low table; which action annoyed Justina unreasonably. Lighting his cheroot, he went on: 'Don't you live in Monteraverde, then, Amalia?'

'No.' She shook her head. 'My family moved to the United States some time ago.'

'I see.' He smiled through a haze of smoke. 'What part of the States do you come from? I know the west coast quite well.'

Justina stared at him in amazement, but Amalia noticed nothing amiss. 'Oh, do you?' She smiled. 'That's interesting. We live near Santa Barbara.'

'Santa Barbara. Oh, yes. I spent some time in Los Angeles.'

'Did you really?' Amalia was fascinated, but Justina was beginning to feel rather sick.

'Amalia—was just leaving,' she began, but Amalia herself interrupted her.

'Yes, I was, but I was trying to persuade your wife to accept an invitation for you both for dinner tomorrow evening. I'm sure my aunt would love to meet you—both.'

Andrew glanced at Justina. 'That sounds interesting,' he remarked. 'There's no reason why we shouldn't accept, is there, *darling*?'

Justina clenched her fists impotently by her sides. 'I don't know whether I ought to leave Tia Renata—'

'Oh, I'm sure Nurse Gomez can cope for a couple of hours,' said Andrew, with annoying complacence. 'And you haven't been out at all—since we arrived.'

Justina was powerless to find any reasonable excuse, and she forced the smile to her lips. 'All—right, Amalia. Thank you, we'd—love to come.'

'Oh, marvellous!' Amalia was enthusiastic. 'About eight?'

'Fine.' Andrew nodded, and she moved reluctantly towards the door again. Justina had the feeling that were she to repeat her invitation to lunch, Amalia would decide to accept. She was obviously having second thoughts now that she had met Justina's husband. Justina wondered exasperatedly why that knowledge should irritate her as much as it did.

Amalia had driven up to the *castelo* in a Landrover, the most usual form of transport in this area, and her chauffeur, a young Monteraverdian, was waiting for her at the wheel. She waved as they drove away and Justina closed the door rather heavily, wishing she did not have to go back into the lounge to confront her adopted husband.

But of course, she had to do just that, and straightening she crossed the hall again.

Andrew was not alone. Juana was with him. She was seated in her usual position by the window, sewing, and Justina wasn't sure whether to feel relieved or otherwise. She had wanted to speak to Andrew. She had wanted to question him about his knowledge of the United States, but perhaps it was as well not to appear too eager. He might become suspicious if she questioned him too closely about his past, and besides, the last thing she wanted was to revive some latent spark of his real identity.

But in spite of that, she was curious herself to know how he could recall being in any particular place, and she wondered how she could broach the subject with Doctor Ramirez next time he came to see her aunt.

As she entered the lounge, Andrew was bending to stub out his cheroot in an onyx ashtray, but he glanced up at her appraisingly, his eyes annoyingly insolent.

'What a pleasant surprise,' he remarked mockingly. 'I'm so glad I came back early and met our unexpected guest!'

Justina made no response, merely linking her fingers together and wandering over to the window, and he went on:

'Have you known Amalia long, Justina?'

She continued to stare unseeingly out of the window, trying to curb her rising impatience. What was there about this man that infuriated her so?

'We went to school together,' she replied slowly at last.

'Really.' He strolled lazily across the room to join her, and she moved further into the window embrasure. 'I thought she was about the same age as you. Is she married?'

Justina glanced across at Juana's impassive face, and then looked annoyedly at the man by her side. 'Does it matter?'

He glanced across at Juana now, and half smiled a slow rather mocking smile. 'Don't be like that, Justina,' he murmured, loud enough for Juana to hear. 'I was only curious. You have no reason to be jealous, my love!'

Justina glared at him. 'I'm not jealous!' she snapped, and then bent her head as Juana looked up in surprise. 'Excuse me! I must wash my hands before lunch.'

'Of course.' He inclined his head and stood aside politely as Justina walked out of the room. She was impotent against his deliberate provocation, and she wished with all her heart that there had been no need to begin this charade. And Amalia's unexpected appearance was going to make things even more complicated.

The following morning Doctor Ramirez arrived to see Renata. The old lady submitted to his ministrations impatiently, and then, glancing across the room at Justina, she said:

'Have you met my niece's husband, Antonio?'

'Of course.' Ramirez straightened, putting his stethoscope back into his case. 'You asked me that the last time I was here.'

Renata frowned. 'Did I? Did I?' She shook her head. 'Then you must forgive the absentmindedness of an old woman. What do you think of him?'

'Please, Tia Renata!' Justina was aghast.

'You mind your own business, young woman, I want to know what my doctor thinks of my nephew-in-law.'

Ramirez gave Justina a reassuring smile. 'I like him,' he answered truthfully. 'Don't you?'

'I'm asking the questions, young man!' Renata could be annoyingly direct when she chose. 'But yes, since you ask, I do. I can't imagine why Justina has so much trouble with him.'

Ramirez frowned. 'Trouble?' he repeated.

'Oh, Tia Renata, please!' exclaimed Justina again.

'Be quiet, Justina. Yes, trouble, Antonio. If there hadn't been trouble, there would have been babies by now. I can't understand it. I should have thought Justina would have liked a child!'

Ramirez looked a little discomfited. 'Surely affairs like these are none of our business, *senhora*?' he murmured discreetly, much to Justina's relief.

'Of course they're my business,' snapped Renata. 'There are too many marriages these days that are little more than the legalisation of sex. I want Justina's to be a proper marriage. I want to know she's with child before I die!'

'*Tia Renata!*' Justina was horrified, and even Ramirez was moving a trifle awkwardly towards the door.

'What's the matter? Have I shocked you? You young people today! You talk so arrogantly about your freedom of speech, and yet you shy away from the truth like so many frightened sheep! Pah! I have no time for you.'

Nurse Gomez moved forward. 'You must not excite yourself, *senhora*,' she said gently.

'I'm not exciting myself!' Renata was petulant. 'Oh, go away and leave me alone, the lot of you! I'm tired. I want to sleep!'

Outside in the corridor, Justina faced the doctor with unhappy eyes. 'How—how is she, doctor?' she asked quietly.

Ramirez shrugged. 'Who can tell? There are times when I think she is weakening, and others, like now, when I am not so sure. The will is there. I am afraid it is a case of the spirit being willing but the flesh is weak.' He bit his lip and touched her shoulder reassuringly. 'Don't take any notice of what she says, Justina. She is only eager for your happiness, that is all.'

'Happiness!' exclaimed Justina bitterly.

'What is wrong?' Ramirez was concerned, and Justina had to gather herself hastily.

'Why, nothing at all. I—I guess I'm just allowing anxiety to get the better of me.'

'Are you sure that's all it is?' Ramirez looked doubtful.

'What else could there be?'

'This man—your husband: all is well?'

'As well as can be expected, I suppose. He—he hasn't remembered anything, of course.'

'No.' Ramirez looked frowningly towards his polished shoes. 'Nothing at all, eh?'

Justina hesitated. 'Well, there was something I wanted to ask you.'

Ramirez looked up, his eyes alert. 'Go on!'

'Well, it's nothing really.' Justina coloured again. 'It's just that I wanted to ask you whether it was possible for him to remember actual places that he had visited.'

'Places?' Ramirez considered. 'Yes, I suppose that's possible. Why? Has he remembered some place? Should I speak with him about it?'

'Oh, no!' Justina was quick to negate this suggestion. 'No, I wouldn't like to—raise unnecessary hopes.'

'Of course.' The doctor nodded. 'That might be unkind. But you think he has remembered something?'

Justina swallowed hard. 'Well, it was just something he said that made me—wonder.'

'I see.' Ramirez began to walk towards the stairs and she walked with him. 'Well, I would suggest you observe his condition closely, and if you suspect him of recalling anything—anything at all, let me know.'

'Yes. Yes, I will, doctor.' Justina nodded, and smiled before preceding him downstairs.

But after he had gone, and the heavy door was closed behind him, she began to wonder exactly what Andrew could remember. Had he not noticed what he had said when Amalia was here? Had the mention of California rung any bells in his subconscious? And if so, was there any likelihood of his real identity returning?

She broke out in a cold sweat at the thought of this possibility. It was one thing to talk blithely to Luis about offering the man money to forget everything that had happened, and quite another to put it into practice. And knowing the man she called Andrew, as she was beginning to, she was not at all certain he would agree to such a suggestion. He might demand a much more gruelling recompense.

She made her way up to her room on slightly unsteady legs. Suddenly everything seemed too much for her, and she flung herself upon the bed and allowed the hot tears to burn her cheeks.

She did not go down to lunch, and when Juana came to her door to ask if there was anything she wanted, she pretended not to hear. The last thing she wanted was for Juana to see her in this state, and perhaps relay it all to her aunt. Even so, by late afternoon, she knew she would have to make the effort and leave her room, and bypassing the lounge she left the *castelo* by the rear entrance and made her way to the stables.

Anton saddled her horse at her request and mounted up himself to accompany her.

'I'd rather be alone,' she said, glad of the dark glasses which hid the faintly swollen lids of her eyes, a legacy from her breakdown earlier.

Anton hesitated. 'It is not right that the *senhora* should ride alone,' he insisted.

'Oh, very well.' Justina had no heart to argue, and with Anton just behind her she cantered out of the courtyard and down the sloping track to the lush greenery of the meadow below.

The sun was slowly sinking behind the mountains, but it was still warm, and the air was fresh with the scent of wild flowers. Flocks of birds, startled from their resting in the trees, rose as they rode beneath the clumps of jacarandas and pine trees, casting moving shadows across the surface of the river that ran deep along the valley floor.

They rode for fully half an hour before turning for home and then Justina gave the mare her head and allowed her to take her own pace. They galloped across the stretch of grassland bordering the river, and then began the ascent up to the *castelo*. The sun was almost gone now, and it was cooler, and Justina felt as though her head was a little clearer, although she was no nearer to finding a solution for the many problems that beset her.

As they reached the gates of the *castelo*, a figure emerged to stand, motionless, watching them make the final ascent to the entrance. Hands on hips, an open-necked white sweat shirt contrasting sharply with the tan of his skin, his identity was unmistakable, and Justina's nerves tautened.

As she reached him, he leant forward and caught the mare's bridle, bringing the animal to a standstill. Stroking its muzzle with a soothing hand, he looked up at Justina questioningly.

'Where have you been?'

Justina held her shoulders straight. 'Riding,' she replied, unnecessarily.

'I can see that. I asked where?'

'Nowhere in particular. Why?'

'I was concerned about you. Juana said you had no lunch.'

'I wasn't hungry.' Justina moved impatiently. 'Can I go now?'

'In a moment.' He gestured that Anton should enter the courtyard and leave them. 'You seem to have something on your mind, Justina. What is it?'

She sighed. 'Will you please let go of my bridle,

and allow me to dismount? It's getting late and I need to bathe and change.'

'Oh, yes. Before our dinner engagement. Well, so do I. Is that what's worrying you?'

'Of course not.' Justina dug her heels into the mare's sides and she whinneyed protestingly. 'Please, get out of my way.'

He shrugged and stepped back, releasing the animal, and she cantered into the courtyard. Sliding from the mare, she was about to march into the *castelo* when he came behind her and caught her wrist.

'One more thing,' he said, and as she turned he slid the dark glasses from her nose, exposing her eyes which were still slightly red-rimmed. 'Well, well,' he observed mockingly. 'What is all this about?'

Justina glared at him furiously. As always he had her at a disadvantage. How could it be? How could he, a man without any recollections except those she had placed in his mind, constantly achieve this kind of disconcertment with her? Surely the strength of her position as opposed to his should be sufficient to swing the pendulum the other way, but it didn't. Instead, she was always on the defensive.

'Will you please leave me alone?' she cried angrily, trying to free her wrist without much success. 'I've told you, I don't like being touched!'

'Yes, I have gathered that,' he remarked dryly. 'However, there are occasions when your wishes are subject to those of your husband, are there not?'

'What do you mean?'

'I mean that I want to know why you have been crying.'

'It's no business of yours!' she snapped shortly.

'Everything to do with you is my business!' he replied. 'You made it so when you claimed me from the mission hospital!'

Justina stared at him. 'Wh—what do you mean?'

His eyes narrowed. 'What do you think I mean?'

She faltered, 'I don't know.'

'Don't you?' He raised her wrist and looked at its narrow fragility with twisted lips. 'What could I mean, do you suppose? Only that, as I'm your husband, I surely have some rights, if not the ultimate one.'

She stared at him, her face burning. 'It—it's nothing,' she denied. 'Please—let me go!'

He stared at her for a moment longer, his grey eyes boring into hers so that she felt something move unwillingly inside her at that devastating appraisal. 'All right.' He dropped her wrist. 'Go!'

Justina hesitated a moment longer. His abrupt rejection frightened her almost as much as the strangeness of his words. Was he beginning to be suspicious? Was her attitude arousing curiosity inside him?

Oh, she would have to be more careful—more acquiescent.

But her relationship with Andrew—the real Andrew, that was—had not prepared her for a normal relationship with any man, and it was impossible for her to relax with this man under any circumstances.

She turned and walked quickly into the *castelo*, running up the stairs to her room as the desire for escape inspired the need for urgent action.

It wasn't until she had shed her clothes and sought the scented sanctuary of her bath that she recalled the feelings he had aroused within her only a few moments ago. There was something wholly disturbing about that realisation, and she ran smoothing soapy fingers across the skin of her wrist which he had so cruelly bruised by that violent clasp. And yet a strange sliver of anticipation ran down her spine at the remembrance, and it was not hatred that turned the muscles of her lower limbs to sudden compliance.

She took a choking breath. She was being stupid, crazily stupid, allowing her senses to be moved by the actions of a man like that, a man like Andrew, no doubt, who found the conquest of women much to his taste.

She thrust the soap aside. Had she forgotten so quickly what came after this weakening of the senses, this dissolving of the emotions? Would she ever forget the brutal act that culminated a man's passions? An act that left a woman cold and empty and utterly distrait.

CHAPTER SEVEN

AMALIA GARCIA'S UNCLE and aunt lived in a large hacienda-type dwelling on the far side of the valley. They were farmers, and although her uncle was now retired his son continued the family concern. They had only had the one child, and as he was now married and with a home and family of his own, they welcomed Amalia back into their midst almost as though she was their daughter.

Justina and the man she called Andrew drove across the valley by the light of the moon that had pushed its way through lowering clouds. The calm weather seemed about to break, and occasionally spots of rain splashed the windscreen of the Landrover. Andrew was driving, and Justina thought, with a rising sense of the hysterical ridiculous, that it would have been the last straw if it had turned out that this man could not drive after she had announced that he was used to racing cars.

She had taken a great deal of trouble with her appearance, taking care to eliminate all traces of the tears she had shed earlier, and she was comfortably aware that her gown of emerald velvet complemented the dull-gold brilliance of her hair.

Tia Renata had been delighted to learn that they were going out together, seeing this as a further sign of their compatibility, but she would have been less pleased if she had been aware that the journey to Amalia's aunt's house was accomplished almost in complete silence. An awful wall of unspoken anger was growing between them, and Justina had no idea of how to destroy it without destroying herself in the process.

When they reached the house, they found that the other guests had already arrived. Amalia herself greeted them at the door, looking startlingly beautiful in a gown of blue chiffon which moulded the slim lines of her figure with loving closeness.

'Justina, *amada*,' she exclaimed, in her husky voice, speaking in English for Andrew's benefit. 'And Andrew!' Her eyes grew warm. Tucking an arm through each of theirs, she went on: 'Come along. We've been waiting for you. I'll introduce you to everyone, and then they can serve dinner. I'm ravenous, aren't you?'

There were three guests besides themselves, as well as Amalia's uncle and aunt, and Amalia herself. Justina knew the Nobres, Amalia's relatives, but the others were only vaguely familiar. It was strange how one could live so near people without actually getting to know them, she thought, but she supposed Tia Renata's desire for seclusion was mainly responsible for their lack of communication.

Of the guests, there was a middle-aged couple by the name of Hernandez, and a young man, a friend of Amalia's, introduced as Vasco Domingos. Obviously he had been invited to make up the numbers, but as he attached himself to Justina after their introduction, it meant that Amalia had Andrew all to herself.

To begin with, Justina was slightly disconcerted by the young man's attentions, not wishing to offend Amalia by responding to his flattery, but as the evening wore on, she began to wonder whether the whole thing hadn't been planned beforehand. She didn't know Amalia, the *mature* Amalia, that well, but it certainly seemed that she found Justina's husband quite fascinating.

But what of it? she asked herself impatiently. He was nothing to her, whatever he imagined, and if he thought to make her jealous by encouraging Amalia to flirt with him, he was going to be disappointed. Even so, it rankled, and because it did, Justina paid more attention to Vasco Domingos than she would otherwise have dreamed of doing.

At dinner she found herself seated between her host and Vasco, while Andrew was opposite between Amalia's aunt and Amalia herself. Conversation was general mostly, and mainly English, but when it did occasionally lapse into Portuguese Amalia took pleasure in explaining what had been said to her companion.

During the course of the meal, which Justina did little justice to, she learned that Vasco lived in Queranova. His father was the manager of a bank there and Vasco himself was newly out of college. Queranova was on the coast, and when he began to tell Justina about his interest in skindiving, she became absorbed in spite of herself. Her life with Andrew had been spent in the major cities of Europe, and his idea of having a good time did not encompass any kind of physical activity.

'You know there are many wrecks of Spanish vessels still lying undisturbed on the ocean floor,' Vasco said, with enthusiasm. 'It is my dream that one day I will discover such a wreck, filled with gold bullion, and silver plate, and jewels...' He smiled. 'I would be a rich man.'

'Oh, but I thought treasure trove had to be declared or something,' exclaimed Justina.

'It does. But as you know, the value of such things is rising all the time. When a wreck is discovered it has to be first decided to whom it belongs, and then, when this is accomplished, a price is negotiated between the government involved and the discovery team.'

'I see.' Justina smiled. 'It sounds fascinating.'

'It is. Apart from anything else, the actual diving is very exciting. You have no idea of the beauty that lies beneath the surface of our reefs and lagoons.'

'I hope you are not trying to persuade Justina to

join one of your expeditions, Vasco!' Amalia's laugh-
ing voice broke into their conversation. 'I somehow
cannot see her donning a rubber suit and oxygen cyl-
inders.'

'Why not?' Justina looked across at the other girl
challengingly. 'Why shouldn't I?'

Amalia raised her narrow dark eyebrows, glancing
sideways at the man at her side. 'I would not have
thought it was your style, that is all, *amada*. You do
not strike me as being one of these sporting types.'

'Perhaps my wife has hidden talents,' drawled the
man opposite Justina mockingly. 'In any event, I
agree with Amalia, I do not think you would find such
activity to your liking.'

'I disagree.' Justina turned back to Vasco. 'Have
you ever dived in the lake, here in the valley?'

Vasco shook his head. 'No. The lake is too deep,
too cold. I prefer warmer waters. Just recently we
were diving in the Caribbean, to the north of the Ba-
hamas, and that was ideal.'

'And do you really think there are ships—treasure
ships—waiting to be discovered?' Andrew asked, ignoring for the moment Amalia's efforts to draw his
attention back to her.

Vasco looked across at his questioner. 'Oh, without
doubt,' he replied at once. 'There are many, many
vessels still unaccounted for. And most of them con-
tain treasure of some sort. You must remember that
the Spanish conquerors intended to bring all their val-

uables with them: gold plate, silver plate, coins, jewels. They were without doubt the richest settlers any land could hope to have.'

'And I suppose a lot of what they brought will have been ruined by sea-water,' nodded Andrew thoughtfully. 'Books, records, that kind of thing.'

'Of course. And clothes, too. Spanish ladies wore gowns encrusted with jewels, completely priceless to a museum.'

Andrew nodded again. 'I agree. It is fascinating.' He looked at Justina. 'However, I must also agree with Amalia that such exploration is not for you.'

Justina's fingers gripped the edge of the table tightly. 'I didn't say it was. Nevertheless, I should like to learn to dive.' She looked at Vasco. 'Perhaps you could teach me.'

'If you need to learn, I will teach you,' snapped the man she had claimed to be her husband, and Justina's lips parted.

'You *know*—how—how to skin-dive?' she faltered faintly.

Amalia's eyes widened mockingly. 'Didn't you know, *amada*?'

'No. No, I didn't.' Justina looked nervously at the man opposite, but he seemed completely indifferent to her anxiety.

'Why should you?' he countered. 'The situation has never arisen, has it? Until now.'

Justina looked down at her plate. What little appetite she had had, had completely evaporated, and she pushed the plate aside and sought the wine in her glass with slightly unsteady fingers. What did he mean by saying he knew how to skin-dive? her brain buzzed wildly. Had he remembered something else? Was his memory returning in these little bits and pieces? Like saying he knew the west coast of the United States the day before?

After the meal was over, they all adjourned to the lounge for coffee, and Amalia played some records, Justina found herself beside Senhora Nobre, Amalia's aunt, and when the elderly woman began asking about Justina's aunt, she was grateful for the opportunity to escape the chaos of her thoughts for a while.

Andrew was talking to Senhor Hernandez across the room, but from time to time Justina was conscious of his eyes upon her, and she could not help but wonder what he was thinking. It was strange to speculate on the emptiness of a mind without recollection.

Amalia opened the tall french windows which gave on to a small patio and suggested they should dance. When Andrew showed no sign of complying, she roped in Vasco, and they moved slowly to the strains of some one time famous orchestra. Justina was more accustomed to the magnetic, drugging beat music which Andrew had always enjoyed, but it was quite pleasant sitting in the cool of the evening, sipping a liqueur and listening to the rustle of the night animals in the shrubs beyond the patio.

'Do you expect to stay long with your aunt?' Senhora Nobre was asking, and Justina tried to concentrate on what was being said.

'I'm not sure,' she temporised, unable to put any time limit on the length of her deception. 'Until my aunt is better, I hope.'

Senhora Nobre nodded. 'I expect it was quite a surprise when Amalia appeared the other day.'

Justina smiled. 'It was. It's so long since I'd seen her.'

'Yes.' Senhora Nobre glanced to the patio where her niece was presently attempting to teach Vasco one of the more modern variations of dancing. 'I am so glad to see her looking happy again. She has had such an unhappy time recently.'

'Oh?' Justina frowned. 'She didn't say anything to me.'

'No. No, she wouldn't. But it happens that way sometimes.' Senhora Nobre sighed. 'There was this man, you see. A most respectable man by all accounts, and Amalia fell madly in love with him. If you know her at all, you will know that she can be intensely absorbed in what she is doing, and that was how it was with this man.' Senhora Nobre shook her head sadly. 'Unfortunately, he was married, with a family. Amalia did not know this, of course. She was expecting to become betrothed, married, even. But what happened?' Senhora Nobre spread her hands.

'He grew tired of Amalia, and he went back to his wife, of course.'

'Oh!' Justina bit her lip. 'I'm sorry,' she added, inadequately.

Senhora Nobre played absently with the string of pearls about her throat. 'Yes, it was most unfortunate, most unfortunate! Amalia is such a nice girl—such a good girl! It would never occur to her that this man might be playing—what is it, you say?—fast and loose, yes?'

'Yes.' Justina frowned. 'He was an American?'

'I believe so. But of Latin descent. Most suitable in every way. Poor Amalia! It must have been a terrible shock.'

'Yes,' said Justina again, looking once more towards the patio. Amalia had abandoned her attempts to teach Vasco steps which were obviously alien to him, and had joined Andrew and Senhor Hernandez, joining in their conversation with a complete lack of regard for their privacy.

Justina sighed. Amalia did not look heartbroken, but maybe she was being uncharitable. Certainly she was hiding it well if she was.

'It must be nice to be so happily married yourself,' Senhora Nobre was saying now. 'I expect Amalia envies you.'

Justina managed a faint smile. So far as her relationship with the man she called Andrew was concerned, the least said the better. To her relief, Senhor

Nobre came to join them at that moment, and he, too, began questioning her about her aunt and satisfactorily leaving the problems of her marriage alone.

She was inordinately glad when it was time for them to take their leave. Vasco had spent the last quarter of an hour before their departure trying to persuade her to agree to go riding with him within the next few days, but although he suggested they could make up a foursome with Amalia and her husband, Justina was not keen. For the moment, she had had quite enough of Amalia's company.

When the lights of the Nobre house disappeared behind them, Justina curled her fingers inside one another and said: 'Why did you say you could skindive?'

Andrew didn't take his eyes from the road ahead, his long brown fingers sliding over the wheel expertly. 'Was there any reason why I should not?'

'No. Except that you don't.' Justina was tense.

'Don't I?' He glanced her way now and she was glad of the darkness to hide the heat of her cheeks.

'No. Did you think you did?'

He expelled his breath in a lazy sigh. 'Not necessarily.'

'Then why did you say it?'

His lips twisted wryly. 'Because no pretty Spanish boy is going to teach my wife to do anything!' he retorted shortly.

Justina had expected many things, but not that. She stared at him in amazement. 'What did you say?'

'You heard me,' he remarked dryly. 'I may not have a memory, but I'm not a fool!'

Justina was astounded. 'How dare you criticise my actions after the way you've behaved this evening?' she snapped.

Then she bit her lip furiously. She had not meant to say that. She had not intended that he should know that she had noticed anything he had been doing. But it was said now, and there was no taking it back.

'So,' he said mockingly. 'You are jealous.'

'I am not jealous,' she refuted angrily. 'I just object to you thinking you have any right to direct my activities.'

'But I do have the right,' he contradicted her, with cool assurance. 'You're my wife, and damn you, you'll remember it!'

Justina stared at him through a mist of violent indignation, but short of exposing herself there was no retort she could make. 'I—I don't recall your ever feeling so strongly about it before,' she murmured tremulously, realising something was expected of her.

His fingers tightened round the wheel for a moment. 'Don't you? But then I have the feeling our marriage was not all it should have been before the plane crash.'

'What do you mean?' Her eyes darted to his face.

'It's obvious, isn't it? We don't exactly act like a loving couple, do we?'

Justina pressed the palms of her hands to her cheeks. 'I've explained—'

'Oh, no, you haven't. Not satisfactorily, at least.' His voice was harder now. 'You can't expect me to accept everything you say without question, can you? After all, I'm only hearing one side of the argument.'

Justina swallowed hard. She was getting into deep water and had no idea how to extricate herself. 'You're talking as though our behaviour is not exactly the same as thousands of other couples. You may not be aware of the fact, but the ideal marriage is far from commonplace in the so-called civilised world!'

He glanced obliquely at her. 'You're saying that ours was not an ideal marriage?'

Justina flushed. 'Oh, must we continue with this ridiculous conversation—'

'I think we must. I have the right to know where I stand.'

Justina's breast was rising and falling rapidly beneath the soft material of her gown. 'Oh, please,' she exclaimed. 'I'm tired. I—I don't know how to answer you.'

'The truth might be a good idea,' he remarked dryly.

'What do you mean?'

'Just what I say. If our relationship was unsatisfactory, I should be told, shouldn't I?'

'Oh, I see.' Justina bent her head. For a moment she had thought his memory had returned. Gathering her crumbling defences, she went on: 'What does it matter anyway? At the moment, we might just as easily be strangers.'

'But we're not strangers, are we? We're husband and wife and somehow I don't find your explanations very reassuring.' He narrowed his eyes. 'Particularly as you obviously object to my showing any interest in another woman.'

Justina looked up indignantly. 'What you do is of complete indifference to me!' she burst out, and then regretted the impulse to retaliate like that, not least because of the realisation that it was not entirely true.

'Indeed,' he remarked, with the kind of complacence that discomfited her. 'Then why did you marry me?'

His tanned fingers swung the steering wheel so that the Landrover fitted its width between the narrow struts of the wooden bridge which spanned the river at its narrowest point. The wheels echoed hollowly above the surging waters, and then they were across and mounting the slope on the opposite bank. The moon was hidden now by clouds, and the rain which had threatened earlier suddenly began to fall in torrents, drenching the windscreen and forcing him to put the wipers into operation. A chill wind seemed to appear from nowhere, adding its own touch of eeriness to an already unnerving situation. Justina wished they were home, she had never ceased thinking of the *castelo* as home, and she longed for the security and sanctuary of her own room there.

But they were not home, they were here, still over a mile from their destination, and he was asking the one question she had dreaded him asking.

'Well?' he said, cursing as the wheels spun for a moment on a particularly hazardous dip in the track. 'Why did you? Did you love me?'

'I—yes—yes, of course I loved you.' Justina pressed the palms of her hands together tightly.

He drew his brows together in a deep frown. 'I notice you said *loved*. Do I take it you no longer love me?'

Justina made a helpless gesture. This was an impossible situation. 'How do I know?' she cried. 'I've told you—we're like strangers to one another!'

'Whose fault is that?'

'It's no one's fault,' she exclaimed desperately. 'Until—until you regain your memory, there's bound to be a—a rift between us.'

'Is there?' His tone was cold. 'Why? Surely the most natural way to recover that relationship is by behaving in the way any normal husband and wife would behave.'

Justina took a shaking breath. 'All right, all right,' she said unsteadily. 'Ours—ours was not a normal relationship—long—long before the plane crash.' That at least was true.

'I see.' He changed down to negotiate a sharp bend in the road. 'Now that sounds much more like it. But why? What caused our relationship to deteriorate in such a way?'

Justina bit her lip. She hated this. She hated having to discuss her most personal and private affairs with this man who was a stranger to her. It was all right for him. He imagined he was hearing about *his* life. Only she knew that he had had nothing to do with that life before she had decided he should.

'Must we revive all the old hatreds?' she asked appealingly. 'Couldn't we just leave things the way they are? At least, until it begins to mean something to you?'

'But it does mean something to me now,' he said, shocking her into a startled gasp.

'What do you mean?'

'I mean that I recall there being trouble. I recall marital strife; oh, yes, definitely, that means something to me.'

Justina was horrified. What did it mean? Was he beginning to remember his own life to the extent that he recalled being married? Or was it simply a case of familiarity with her affairs breeding its own kind of fictitious memories? She had no way of knowing, but the idea that he might be a married man knocked her sick and cold. Was it possible he had a wife? And if so, why hadn't she come forward to find his whereabouts after she learned of the plane crash? Or didn't she know yet?

She was trembling as she said: 'What—what exactly do you remember?'

He frowned with assumed concentration. 'Very little, I'm afraid. But I do recall rows between us. Was there another man?'

Justina stiffened. '*No!*'

'No?' He shook his head thoughtfully. 'Another woman, perhaps?'

Justina was a mass of angry recriminations, recriminations she could not voice. How dared he mock her like this? He couldn't recall their life—because he had had no part of it.

'I don't want to talk about it any more,' she snapped fiercely. 'Please! Let's just leave it alone.'

'So there was another woman,' he persisted infuriatingly. 'I wonder why? Your untouchability—your coldness, perhaps!'

Justina glared at him. 'How—how dare you?' she gasped, and without really stopping to consider what she was about to do she moved her hand as if to slap him across his mocking face, causing him to recoil automatically and the Landrover to skid dangerously near the edge of the water-logged track.

'You little bitch!' he snarled fiercely, stepping hard on the brakes and bringing the vehicle to a screeching halt. With a muffled cry she thrust open her door and sprang out into the rain-swept darkness.

She didn't stop to consider the advisability of her actions; pure, unadulterated anger touched with fear were propelling her swiftly away from the cause of that primitive emotion.

Within seconds she was soaked. The semi-tropical storm was nowhere near abating, and as she slid ignominiously down the muddy slope away from the road she lost a sandal and the exquisitely embroidered shawl which had been her only outer covering. She didn't know where she was going, she only sought escape from his anger, and her experiences with Andrew Douglas crowded back into her mind to terrify her further. She could still feel the wetness of his soft mouth on hers and feel horror at his greedy hands on her body.

'*Mae deus*,' she groaned to herself tearfully, reaching the grassy bank below and running wildly across its slippery surface.

Then she heard him calling her, his voice harsh and demanding through the lashing whip of the rain against her face. 'Justina! Justina, for God's sake, don't be a fool! Come back! What the hell do you think I'm going to do to you?'

Justina halted, breathless, crouching down in a clump of reeds, panting as coherent thought attempted to gain control of her brain. What was she doing? Running away like this? What had she been afraid of? What could he have done to her?

But at the moment of panic she had been unable to

think coherently. Her nerves had been stretched to breaking point and escape had seemed the only logical solution. But now she was not so sure. Kneeling here in the darkness, her hair lank and soaking about her shoulders, she was inviting pneumonia or worse, and what good would that do? For a brief moment she contemplated what might happen were she to accept such a fate, and then sanity returned. She was crazy allowing this man, this impostor, to hurt her like this. It didn't matter what he thought of her. In a few weeks, a few months at most, he would be gone, and then she could forget this brief episode for ever.

She had been so absorbed with her thoughts she had been unaware that he had found a torch in the Landrover and had climbed down the muddy bank without difficulty and was presently raking the surrounding grassland with its beam, intent on discovering her whereabouts. If she rose to run, he would be bound to notice the movement, and she kept perfectly still, praying he would not notice her. She didn't quite know what she would do if he did not notice her. She supposed she could make her way back to the *castelo* on foot without too much difficulty, but she was going to get terribly chilled in the process.

However, his method of searching was thorough, and she rose defiantly to her feet only seconds before the beam settled itself upon her. She had no desire for him to find her kneeling at his feet.

Immediately he lowered the shaft of light down the length of her body, noticing the way the wet gown moulded her figure, and when he spoke his voice was curiously grim.

'What in hell do you think you're doing?' he snapped. 'For God's sake, woman, you'll catch your death of cold!'

Justina shivered, as much with apprehension as with the dampness of her dress, but he interpreted it differently. Making no attempt to take her, he said: 'Come on! Get back to the Landrover!'

Justina hesitated only a moment before stepping forward, stumbling over the root of a tree and saving herself only narrowly. He made no effort at assistance, and she went past him, her whole being filled with hateful indignation. He was no gentleman, she told herself fiercely. He was just as horrible as the real Andrew had been.

It was difficult to get back up the bank. She found her shoe and the shawl, but they were thick with mud and she couldn't attempt to put them on. Holding them in one hand, she struggled to mount the slope while Andrew, the man she called Andrew, sprang lithely up the bank without any apparent difficulty. She wished he would slip and fall. She wished he was as covered in mud and as ignominiously undignified as she.

'Having problems?' he queried, in a mocking tone, from the top of the bank.

Justina looked up angrily. 'Oh, go away and leave me alone!' she cried, near to tears. Her beautiful dress was ruined, and if she wasn't careful it was going to get torn too.

'As you wish,' he remarked indifferently, and turned away, but she dared not let him go.

'*No*! No, please, give me a hand!' she murmured unhappily.

He regarded her intently in the pale light of the torch, and then without a word he went down on his haunches and offered her his hand. His hand was cool and firm, and it was easy for him to hoist her almost bodily up the bank. She contemplated giving a sudden backward jerk and causing him to measure his length in the mud as well, but she dared not.

Instead, she struggled upwards and reached the top without further incident. The wind was forcing her hair across her face, and she wiped it out of her mouth as she followed him across to the vehicle.

He made no attempt to assist her inside, and wrapping her skirts about her she slid on to the leather seat. He was already inside, and at her seating he set the engine in motion and they moved away.

He said nothing during the short journey to the *castelo*, but she dreaded the moment of arrival when Juana would have to see her and know why she should be in such a state.

However, when they reached the *castelo* he said: 'Stay here. I'll get you a coat. You can go straight up to your room. Come down when you've bathed and changed and I'll have Benita heat some water and I'll make a hot spirit drink for you.'

Justina wanted to refuse. She wanted to brush his offer of assistance aside, but she could not, and so she nodded her head and when he returned with a cape of hers from the hall closet, she wrapped it thankfully about her.

However, it was earlier than they had thought and Juana was still up, and despite Justina's efforts to hasten across the hall and up the stairs to escape notice, the unusual activity brought the elderly companion to the lounge door in her usual silent way, and she stood regarding them with horrified eyes.

'*Senhora!*' she exclaimed, in amazement. 'What has happened? Has there been an accident?' She looked in astonishment at Andrew, but he appeared little discomfited himself, only the shoulders of his dinner jacket and the sparkling drops of water on the thickness of his dark hair bearing witness to the fact that he, too, had been out in the storm.

Justina didn't know what to say. She looked despairingly at Andrew, and without effort it seemed he came to her rescue.

'Senhora Douglas got out of the Landrover to move a wounded marmoset out of the path,' he replied smoothly, 'and unfortunately she stumbled in the darkness. The road was very muddy.'

Juana's eyes widened in disbelief. 'A wounded marmoset, *senhor*?' she echoed faintly.

'That's what I said.' Andrew's eyes bored into hers disconcertingly. 'Why? What did you think had happened? Did you imagine with your innate sense of the romantic that we might have been making love out there in the darkness when the storm broke?'

Juana's face suffused with colour. She was taken aback by the directness of his attack. 'Of course not,' she denied uneasily. 'I—I didn't know what to think, *senhor*.'

'Well, now you do. So perhaps you would be good enough to go to Benita and ask her to heat some water for a hot drink for the *senhora*.'

'*Sim, senhor*.'

Juana was forced to obey, albeit unwillingly, and with a helpless glance at his taut features Justina continued upstairs. It was the first time a man had defended her to anybody, and it was a curiously disturbing experience.

CHAPTER EIGHT

IN HER BEDROOM, Justina stripped off her clothes without thought of intrusion and leaving them in a damp heap on her soft carpet she went into her bathroom. The shower was hot and comforting, and she allowed the soft water to soak her hair, too. Mud clung to it from her encounter with the muddy bank, and it was wonderful to feel clean and sweet smelling once more.

When she was dry, she dressed in a long cream silk hostess gown, that previously had never been worn. Its long classic lines accentuated the slightly voluptuous curves of her body, and she took out a heavy tapestry-woven house-coat in shades of blue and green to wear with it. The housecoat was secured by a broad sash, but was open at the throat to reveal the smooth skin of her throat.

Her hair was still damp, of course. It was too long to dry instantly, but already it was recovering its lustre, and without make-up she looked extraordinarily youthful.

She pondered the advisability of going downstairs again, but knew she had to comply. Besides, no doubt Juana would still be up, eager to hear all the details of Justina's unusual rescue venture.

But to her surprise, when she entered the lamp-lit lounge of the *castelo* she found it completely deserted, only the glowing fire in the grate bearing witness that someone had been here only recently.

She looked round curiously, and was about to pour herself a drink and go when Andrew appeared in the doorway. She saw at once that he had changed, too. He was no longer wearing his dinner clothes, but had put on close-fitting black suede trousers and a crimson silk shirt, opened at the neck. Her nerve ends tingled a little at the sight of him. If he had forgotten that attempted slap earlier, she had not, and she wished for the first time since coming to the *castelo* that Juana would suddenly appear.

But she did not, and he advanced into the room without any particular menace becoming evident. He walked across to the cocktail cabinet with casual familiarity, and Justina saw that a flask of hot water had been placed on the cabinet in readiness. As she watched, he poured a measure of brandy into a glass to which he added a sufficient amount of water from the flask to set it steaming. Then he picked up the glass and carried it across to her, handing it to her without a word.

'Thank you.' Justina took the glass and sipped the fiery liquid experimentally. It burned her throat and she gasped, and then nodded. He turned and went back to the cabinet to pour himself some whisky.

Justina moved awkwardly to the fire, and stood

looking down into its depths. She didn't want to sit down and have him imagine she wanted to prolong this *tête-à-tête*, but conversely her legs seemed incapable of supporting her.

He swallowed his whisky at a gulp, and putting down his glass, he walked across to where she was standing. His height gave him an added advantage, and in the lamplight his shadow looked enormous.

'Well?' he said at last, when she failed to look up. 'Are you recovered from your histrionics?'

Now she looked up. 'I do not indulge in histrionics!' she denied hotly.

'Then what explanation can you give for your behaviour? For God's sake, what made you dash out of the Landrover like a mad thing? What did I do?'

Justina's cheeks burned. 'You—you were indescribably rude to me!' she accused him.

'Was I?' He stood watching her with disturbingly intent eyes, his hands resting lightly on his hips.

Justina sensed the mockery in his voice. 'I suppose you found it all very amusing!' she snapped angrily. 'Causing me to make an idiot of myself—ruining my clothes!'

'You can hardly blame me for your actions,' he remarked reasonably. 'And I suppose it would be amusing—to an outsider.'

Justina sipped her drink impatiently. Sooner or later she always reached frustration point with him. Without effort, he was capable of reducing her to a state of childish retaliation.

Suddenly he put out his hand and gently took a handful of her hair into his fingers. Justina flinched visibly, but this time he did not immediately release her.

'What is it?' he demanded, his eyes darkening between the thick lashes. 'Why do you act this way every time I come near you? Surely my touching your hair isn't a crime! What have I ever done that you should be so terrified of me?'

Justina put up her hand to pull her hair from his grasp, but he would not let go. 'I—I've told you,' she panted chokily. 'Please—let me go!'

He ignored her, his eyes following the length of her body, so lightly concealed by the soft folds of her gown that had parted at the bodice when she raised her hand to free herself. 'You're very beautiful, Justina,' he murmured, almost to himself. 'Too beautiful to be as cold as you pretend to be!'

Justina's heart pounded. 'Let me go!' she commanded impotently, trying to pull herself away from him. 'You're hurting me!'

He took the glass from her free hand and when she would have beat her fist against him, he twisted her arm behind her back, forcing her body close against his so that she could feel every muscle beneath the taut material of his garments. 'Don't fight me!' he said huskily, and bent his head to put his mouth against her throat.

Justina went a little mad, twisting her head from side to side, pressing her other hand against his chest, feeling the sensuous softness of the silk clinging to her fingers, warm from his flesh. She wriggled and struggled against him, but she only succeeded in arousing him further, and when his hand caught and imprisoned her face and his hard mouth parted the softness of hers she felt herself slipping into a vortex of emotional urgency that was like nothing she had ever experienced before.

He kissed her many times, long, disturbing kisses, that robbed her of the desire to escape his demanding sexuality, and only when his fingers slid the cream silk gown from her shoulders exposing the flesh to his searing touch did a trace of remembrance of agonies past bring her to her senses.

With a cry of remorse, she dragged herself away from him, drawing the gown protectively about her, staring at him with tortured eyes. 'How—how dare you?' she gasped, shaking her head tremulously.

He controlled himself with obvious difficulty, leaning against the fireplace, wiping the back of his hand across his mouth. 'How dare I what?' he sneered coldly. 'Make love to my wife? Where's the harm in that?'

Justina turned away. 'I—I'm going to bed,' she said unsteadily.

'A good idea!' he said, with a cruel mockery.

Justina turned, swaying a little. 'What do you mean?'

'That's a favourite expression of yours, isn't it?' he demanded sarcastically. 'What do you think I mean?'

Justina shook her head. 'I—I don't know.'

'Of course you do. I'm a man, Justina, not a tame lap-dog. I want you—and by God, I'm going to have you!'

Her lips parted, and there was terror in her eyes. 'You—you wouldn't!'

'Wouldn't I?' His lips twisted. 'You're forgetting something, Justina. Just now when I held you in my arms, you surrendered to me. You wanted me, just as much as I wanted you. Did you think I wasn't aware of that?'

'That's not true,' she burst out.

'It is true. Don't belittle yourself still further by denying it. But what you seem to overlook is the realisation that you simply cannot respond like that to a man and expect him to go obediently away to his own bed without satisfaction!'

Justina swallowed hard. 'I—I can't help that. All right, all right, I—I did respond—a little. I—I'm sorry.'

He walked towards her slowly. 'Don't be sorry. It's the best thing that could have happened, in the circumstances. Perhaps it's the chance we've been waiting for—the opportunity to resume our lives again as normal human beings.'

'*No!*' Justina held out a hand in front of her as though to ward him off, even while her traitorous senses leapt at the thought that he might take her in his arms again. 'No, you're wrong. I—I'm not ready—'

His eyes narrowed. 'Oh, but you are, Justina!' His fingers curved round her wrist, drawing her inexorably towards him, but even as her breath became pain inside her, there was the sound of hurrying footsteps and Nurse Gomez appeared in the entrance to the lounge, her hair askew, her dressing gown of maroon wool dragged hastily about her shoulders.

'Oh, *senhora*,' she exclaimed, in their own language, '*senhora*, the old *senhora* has had another seizure!'

At once Justina was free and he was saying: 'What did she say?' with impatient grimness.

Justina relayed Nurse Gomez's message, and he raked a hand through his hair. 'The doctor!' he said. 'Ramirez! Can we get in touch with him?'

'Well, there's no telephone!' exclaimed Justina, trembling a little, unable at the moment to think coherently. All she was aware of was the precarious state of her aunt's health, and of how soon they could get assistance.

Nurse Gomez spoke in English now. 'Perhaps the

senhor could fetch the doctor!' she suggested. 'I will go back. She must not be left alone.'

'I'll—I'll come with you!' Justina looked at Andrew with tortured eyes. 'What—what will you do?'

For a brief moment his eyes darkened with remembered passion and then he turned abruptly away. 'I'll go for the doctor as Nurse Gomez says,' he stated firmly, and walked quickly away across the hall to get his coat from the hall closet.

Justina thought she would never forget that night as long as she lived. Apart from its beginnings, which had been devastating enough, there was the agonising wait for Doctor Ramirez and the terrible sound of her aunt's laboured breathing in the silence of that cloistered room. Nurse Gomez busied herself attending to her patient, but all Justina had to do was sit and wait and suffer the rigours of her own thoughts.

If Tia Renata died now, she felt it would be a judgement on herself for her extreme conduct in the face of difficulty, and although she tried to keep thoughts of the man to the back of her brain she could not help but recall the disturbing realisation that she had wanted him to make love to her without caring of the consequences, without caring that their relationship was nothing more than an empty charade. There were even times during that long, lonely night when she even considered putting all thoughts of ever telling him the truth out of her mind. But then she remembered what he had said about recalling marital arguments and her body went cold. Unless he was making the whole thing up at some time he had had a wife. It was not unreasonable. He was a most attractive man, and it was unlikely that some woman should not have ensnared him before now. So what was she to do?

Doctor Ramirez was reassuringly competent. In no time at all he had taken control of the situation and although he endorsed the treatment Nurse Gomez had already given, his presence gave them all confidence. He remained with her aunt for the remainder of the night, and urged Justina to go to bed as there was nothing she could do.

But Justina preferred to stay, just in case. She felt a terrible sense of guilt towards her aunt and she wanted to be there if she should be needed.

Towards dawn, there seemed a slight improvement in Renata's condition. Her breathing became less laboured, and she seemed to be sleeping quite peacefully now. Justina turned anxiously to the doctor, and he patted her hand gently.

'We have been lucky,' he said softly. 'I think the crisis is over. But she is very weak, and it will be some days before she begins to regain her strength. I'm telling you this so that you will not worry unnecessarily.'

'Thank you, doctor.' Justina leant over the old lady

tenderly, and touched her wrinkled cheek. 'I don't know how to thank you.'

Ramirez thrust his instruments away into his bag. 'It's my job,' he said simply.

Justina shook her head slowly. 'It's more than that, isn't it? It's a vocation.'

Ramirez smiled. 'Go along with you. You look exhausted. You must get some sleep. Where's that husband of yours gone? He drove me back here like a madman. I don't think I would have cared to drive at such a pace on such roads had I not known he was an experienced driver.'

Justina bent her head. Here was another example of the impulsiveness of her actions. Without a word, she preceded him out of her aunt's bedroom and down the stairs, but as they reached the bottom, Andrew himself appeared from the lounge to confront them.

'Well?' he asked sharply. 'How is she?'

'She'll live,' said Ramirez calmly. 'But she's very weak. I've just been explaining to Justina that it will be some time before she can be expected to regain her previous strength.' He surveyed the man opposite him intently. 'I gather you haven't been to bed either, Andrew?'

Andrew shook his head. 'No.' He shrugged. 'I'll drive you home, doctor.'

'There's no need. I can take the Landrover and

send one of the boys back with it later. He can bring one of the horses from the clinic, and ride back.'

'It's no trouble,' insisted the other man firmly.

Ramirez sighed. 'Very well.' He turned to Justina. 'And you must get some sleep. Promise me that you will go to bed.'

Justina nodded. 'If you say so, doctor.'

'I do.' Ramirez nodded. 'Very well, Andrew. Let us go.'

Justina went up to her room. She had intended ignoring the doctor's advice and getting dressed, but she stretched out on her bed for a moment wearily, and the next thing she knew there was a knocking at her door and Juana's voice was saying: '*Senhora, senhora*! It is lunch time! Will you come down, or do you want one of the servants to bring it up?'

Justina sat up, horrified, to glance at her wrist watch. It was almost one o'clock. She had slept for more than six hours.

Gathering her scattered thoughts, she slid off the bed and went to open the door. 'I—I'll come down, of course, Juana,' she exclaimed. 'I'm sorry. I must have fallen asleep almost at once.'

Juana folded her hands together. 'The *senhor* asked for you not to be disturbed,' she stated expressionlessly. 'But that was at breakfast time. I felt sure you would want to know how your aunt was getting on as it is lunch-time now.'

'Of course. Of course.' Justina felt terrible, smoothing a hand over the tangled brilliance of her hair. 'How—how is Tia Renata? Have you seen her?'

'*Sim, senhora*, I have seen her. She is still sleeping, of course, but her colour is improving, according to Nurse Gomez.'

Justina breathed a sigh of relief. 'Oh, thank goodness! And thank you, Juana, for waking me. I'll get dressed at once.'

Juana nodded silently, and went away, and Justina closed the door once more. *He* had asked for her not to be disturbed. Why? Surely he didn't care about her after the way she had behaved last night.

After a quick shower, she dressed in close-fitting brown canvas pants and a lemon sleeveless sweater, and securing her hair with a band she went downstairs. Benita was in the lounge, asking Juana when she should serve lunch, and she smiled gently when Justina appeared and transferred the request to her.

'Now—whenever you like,' said Justina easily. 'Where—where is the *senhor*?'

'He went out riding, *senhora*,' Juana replied in her indifferent way. 'He hasn't returned yet. He didn't say whether or not he would be in to lunch.'

'I see.' Justina squashed the traitorous feeling of disappointment that overwhelmed all other emotions. 'Very well, Benita. We'll have lunch now.'

After the meal was over, Justina wandered aimlessly about the *castelo*, unable to relax. The events of the night before, combined with her anxiety over her aunt were disturbing the normal equilibrium she possessed, and she couldn't settle to anything. Where was he? Had he had any sleep at all? And why was she allowing herself to care, one way or the other? After all, what had happened? He had kissed her, that was all. Andrew, the real Andrew, had done much more than that, and she had hated him afterwards. How different was this man that she should be behaving in this way?

But the truth of the matter was that at no time had Andrew Douglas ever disturbed the depths of passion she had known she possessed, whereas last night, this other man, this nameless stranger, had aroused her to an awareness of the delights that can be shared between a man and a woman; and with the insatiable curiosity of the feline she found the most wanton thoughts imaginable disturbing the previously composed reaches of her mind.

Doctor Ramirez arrived about three o'clock to see her aunt. Justina accompanied him upstairs and after his examination which he pronounced satisfactory, they went downstairs again.

'Will you have some coffee, doctor?' she asked, as they reached the hall, and Ramirez nodded.

'Thank you. I'd like that.'

Justina gave her instructions to Benita and then followed him into the lounge. He was standing looking out of the window on to the sweep of the valley, but he turned as she entered and smiled. Juana for once was absent.

'Where's Andrew?'

Justina seated herself in a comfortable armchair and indicated that he should do likewise. 'He's—out,' she said slowly. 'Er—riding.'

'I see,' Ramirez drew out his case of cheroots. 'May I?'

'Of course.' Justina smiled and he lit one carefully, inhaling deeply.

'And how are you?' he asked. 'In yourself, I mean?'

Justina shrugged. 'All right, I suppose.'

'You look tired. Are you sleeping all right?'

Justina flushed. 'Of course. Naturally, last night was rather different.'

'Naturally.' Ramirez surveyed the tip of his cheroot with consideration. 'But you're happy?'

'Why shouldn't I be?' she countered, and was relieved when Benita brought in the tray of coffee.

Once it was poured and the doctor had refused one of the delicate biscuits she proffered, he said: 'You could do with a break, Justina. Away from the *castelo* for a few days.'

Justina gasped. 'Oh—oh, but I couldn't.' She set down her cup heavily. 'Particularly not now that Tia Renata had had this other attack.'

Ramirez shook his head. 'On the contrary, now would be an ideal time. It will be some days before

Renata recognises anybody. She needs rest and sedatives and complete isolation. Your presence here is not necessary.'

Justina stared at him. 'But what if she had another attack?'

'That would indeed be unfortunate. But not likely, I do think. Justina, you're so young, and you've been imprisoned here in the *castelo* for well over a month now. It's not good. You're looking pale, wan, distrait! I shall speak to Andrew!'

'*No!*' Justina was hasty. 'No—no, don't do that.'

'Why not? I am sure he will agree with me—'

'Perhaps he will, but I can't go.'

'Nonsense. There is always Luis. I am sure he and Morgana would be more than happy to see you for a few days. Morgana, particularly, in her depressing state of health.'

Justina rose agitatedly to her feet. 'You don't understand—'

'What don't I understand? That you do not wish to be alone with your husband? Is that it?'

Justina coloured. 'I don't know what you mean.'

'Oh, yes, you do. I sense that all is not well between you two. And I can understand, a little. It is only natural in the circumstances that you should both feel strange with one another. But perhaps in Queranova, with Luis, someone else who knew him before the crash, it may ignite some spark of remembrance.'

Justina shook her head helplessly. 'I don't want to go to Queranova.'

'Then I must insist. I do not wish to have two patients on my hands, and if you do not have a break, Justina, that is exactly what will happen. Your nerves are stretched to the limit. I know this. For heaven's sake, girl, give yourself a chance!'

Justina moved restlessly about the room. 'I—I'll think about it,' she promised unhappily.

Ramirez rose to his feet. 'Very well. And now I must go. There is a child at the hospital I must attend—a boy, only ten years of age. He has tuberculosis of the spine.'

Justina gasped, 'How terrible!'

'Yes, it is. But there you are—that is life.' He patted her shoulder. 'Think carefully about what I have said, Justina. Life is so short. Do not abuse it.'

After he had gone Justina resumed her seat in the lounge. Pouring herself more coffee, she drank it slowly, savouring the relaxation it engendered. The idea of leaving the *castelo* terrified her. Who else might she meet in Queranova who was reputed to know Andrew? What manner of difficulties might she run into there if Ramirez forced them to go? The situation was fast becoming impossible.

Getting up from her seat again, she thrust her coffee cup on to the table and walked across to the window. The view was magnificent, but she derived no pleasure from it. Indeed, she hardly saw it at all until movement away below her attracted her attention. Two riders were heading this way, and although the sun was quite dazzling it was possible to distinguish that one was her husband.

Although it was impossible that he should be able to see her from such a distance, she shrank back against the curtains like a conspirator, and watched them discreetly from between the folds. As they drew nearer she recognised her husband's companion: it was Amalia Garcia.

Justina's stomach muscles tightened painfully. What was Andrew doing with Amalia Garcia? Where had they been, and what was more important, where were they going? Surely he could not be bringing her here—to the *castelo*!

But it certainly seemed that way, and an agonising shaft of jealousy rent its way through Justina's heart. While she had been here, alone, unable to relax, unable to apply herself to anything through worrying about him, he had been with Amalia Garcia, and the realisation was devastating in its destruction.

CHAPTER NINE

WITHOUT WAITING to see them enter the courtyard of the *castelo* Justina hurried swiftly across the room and out into the hall, almost knocking Juana over as she was about to enter the room.

'Good heavens, *senhora*, what is wrong?' she exclaimed, pressing a hand to her throat in alarm.

Justina halted unwillingly. 'I'm sorry, Juana,' she apologised tautly. 'Nothing's wrong. I—I was just going up to my room, that's all.'

'Yes, *senhora*.'

Juana looked sceptical, but she said nothing more and Justina went on her way, mounting the stairs with impulsive haste. She was trembling a little now, and after entering her room she locked the door with slightly unsteady fingers. Then she remembered the communicating door and crossing the room locked that also. Only then did she feel safe, and she seated herself wearily at her dressing table, cupping her chin in her hands and staring at her reflection without pleasure.

She was desperately trying to school herself to be calm, but inside she was a mass of tangled nerves and emotions. How dared he bring that woman here without permission? She overlooked the knowledge that he considered the *castelo* his temporary home, too, and that until a few moments ago she had thought of Amalia as her friend.

But all of a sudden the dark-haired companion of her childhood was no longer a friend, and she despised her for betraying their friendship like this. Last night she had suspected that Amalia found Andrew attractive; now she was certain of it. Amalia's face as she had galloped at his side towards the gates leading into the courtyard had been purely triumphant.

Justina hunched her shoulders. Suddenly she felt hopelessly out of her depth. Despite her years in England, she had none of Amalia's easy sophistication, and for the first time she wished she had.

Standing up, she stripped off the close-fitting pants and sweater, throwing them carelessly to the floor. She would not be available, she decided. When Andrew asked where she was, she would be in bed—resting.

But she could no more relax in bed than she could down-stairs. It was several minutes now since she had slid between the cool sheets and there had been no sound from below. They must have arrived. So where were they? What were they doing? Had Juana told them where she was?

She rolled on to her stomach mutinously. She was behaving childishly, she realised unhappily. And what was worse, she was taking the cowardly way.

Gritting her teeth, she slid out of bed again, and reached for her shreds of underclothing. But even as she did so, she heard sounds in the room next door, and presently Andrew's voice saying: 'Justina! Justina, are you there?'

Justina froze, and then she reached for her dressing gown, pulling it on swiftly before replying with assumed languidity:

'Yes? What do you want?'

The handle of the intercommunicating door turned and too late she remembered she had locked it. 'Justina!' His tone was harder now. 'What's going on?'

Justina hesitated. The last thing she wanted was for him to see her like this after the elegant sophistication of Amalia's riding clothes and the sleek coronet of her hair. Her hair was tousled from the bed, and the dressing gown was not her favourite.

'Nothing's going on, Andrew,' she called back, deciding to try and bluff her way out. 'I'm trying to rest, that's all.'

'Don't give me that! Juana saw you go upstairs not fifteen minutes ago!' He rattled the handle of the door. 'Unlock this door before I break the bloody thing down!'

Justina shivered. 'Go away, Andrew. I want to sleep.'

'Like hell you do! You must have seen us coming. Juana said you dashed upstairs like a wild thing!'

Damn Juana, thought Justina angrily.

'I don't have to do what you tell me!' she retorted now. 'I've told you, I want to rest.'

There was a harsh exclamation and then she heard the sound of his shoulder being propelled against the fine panelling and realised he would do exactly as he had said and break down her door if she did not open it to him.

'Oh, wait!' she called hastily, and reluctantly walked across the room and turned the key in the lock.

Andrew thrust open the door and stood glaring at her angrily. 'Don't ever lock that door against me again,' he muttered, his gaze raking her mercilessly. 'Now! What's going on? Why aren't you dressed?'

Justina endeavoured to keep cool. 'I—I tried to explain. I'm tired. I was resting.'

His eyes narrowed. 'Why? Why now? You did see us coming, didn't you?'

Justina pretended to look surprised. 'Us? Who is—us?'

'Don't play games with me, Justina. You know damn nicely Amalia is downstairs.'

'Amalia? Is she? How nice!' Justina turned her back on him and walked with deliberate steps across the room. 'Where did you meet her? Or was it arranged?'

She heard his swiftly drawn breath and for a moment her heart palpitated at the thought that he might take this opportunity to finish what he had started the night before. But he did not, and a moment later the door of the room banged heavily behind him.

Justina quivered. He had gone. And she had been to blame. If he rode away with Amalia now she would be responsible.

With shaking fingers she unfastened the gown and threw it on her unmade bed, dressing with distressing haste, putting on the pants and sweater she had worn earlier. She refused to seek other clothes in an effort to out-shine Amalia's soignée perfection, and only stopped to brush her hair into some semblance of order before going downstairs.

They were in the lounge. She could hear Amalia's tinkling laugh long before she reached the bottom of the stairs, and her heart twisted painfully. Then she straightened her shoulders and marched across the hall and into the tapestry-hung apartment.

Benita had brought them afternoon tea, probably at Andrew's instigation, she thought, and Amalia was charmingly pouring it out. But she looked up in surprise at Justina's appearance and said:

'You're up! Andrew has just told me you were in bed, resting.'

Justina managed not to look into the man's cold face and advanced into the room casually, tugging a strand of hair. 'I was. But when I heard that you had arrived I couldn't stay upstairs, could I? I mean—that wouldn't have been polite, would it?'

Amalia raised her dark eyebrows. 'So long as you

feel up to it, *amada*,' she remarked smoothly. 'Now, Andrew, how many lumps?'

Justina pressed her lips together 'I'll do that, Amalia. We can't have a—guest—pouring tea here. Not when the mistress of the house is about.'

Amalia's expression changed to one of malice. 'Are you the mistress of the house, *amada*? I would have thought that was your aunt's domain.'

Justina forced herself to remain calm, and seated herself determinedly beside the tea tray. 'Well, I suppose it is really,' she admitted, 'but while Andrew and I are here, and Tia Renata is so ill, naturally I assume her duties. Isn't that so, darling?'

She looked up at Andrew now and saw the sudden brilliance of anger in his eyes as he noted her deliberate use of the endearment. For a brief moment, fear invaded her system, and then dispersed again. She must not allow him to intimidate her like this.

'How is your aunt, then?' Amalia enquired at last, obviously deciding there was nothing to be gained by arguing.

'A little better, thank you,' replied Justina. 'Doctor Ramirez came again this afternoon and he seems to think she is improving.'

'Thank God!' said Andrew fervently.

'Yes, indeed.' Amalia managed a faint smile. 'When Andrew told us how he had to drive through that ghastly storm to fetch the doctor we were all most impressed, weren't we, Andrew?'

Justina pressed her lips together, annoyed by Amalia's attempt to bracket them together, and she waited to see what Andrew's response would be.

'The storm was not so bad,' he said deprecatingly. 'I've driven in worse storms in my time.'

'Have you?' Amalia was enthusiastic. 'I suppose when you drove on the motor-racing circuits you had to drive in all weathers.'

'Indeed we did,' he agreed, nodding, and Justina stared at him in amazement. When had Amalia learned about his motor-racing days?

'I remember one occasion,' he went on, 'when I was racing in Belgium—' but Justina had had enough. Her nerves were tingling.

'I don't think Amalia wants to hear about your racing experiences right now, Andrew,' she interjected quickly. 'Er—tell me, Amalia, how did you happen to run into my—husband?'

Amalia hesitated for a moment, and then she said abruptly: 'I met him when I was out riding this morning. He came back and had lunch with us, didn't you, Andrew?'

Justina looked again at him. 'Is that right, Andrew? We—that is, Juana and myself—expected you back for lunch.'

Andrew's dark eyes were veiled by the long lashes. 'Did you? I thought you might appreciate the opportunity to sleep—after last night.' He looked at her squarely and she felt the disturbing lick of passion ignite her senses.

Colouring, she bent her head to attend to the tea cups, praying no one would notice, but she knew he had and that a faint sneer of mockery was lifting the corners of his mouth.

How she hated him in that moment! In spite of everything, in spite of his amnesia, his provocation, his lack of background, he was capable of hurting her more deeply than anyone, man or woman, had ever been able to do. And why? What was there about him that could upset her so?

Squaring her shoulders, she looked up. 'When do you expect to return to the States, Amalia?'

Amalia was taken aback. 'I'm not sure. My father expects his business in Brazil to be over in a week or so. I may go back with him—or—' her eyes lingered on Andrew for a moment '—or I might stay on with my aunt and uncle. They'd like me to.'

'I see.' Justina piled the cups on to the tray. 'It must be lonely for you, though.'

'Why should it be lonely?' Amalia sounded scornful. 'While you and Andrew are here! And there's always Vasco, of course. By the way, he was quite taken with you, wasn't he, Justina? I've never known him behave like that before.'

Justina forced her colour to remain normal. 'I'm sure you're exaggerating, Amalia. Besides, what would I want with a man like him? I have Andrew!'

Amalia's lips tightened. 'Yes,' she drawled. 'So you do.'

Andrew seemed to grow tired of this baiting, for he rose to his feet, glancing at his watch pointedly. 'It's getting late, Amalia. I'll ride part of the way back with you.'

Justina rose too. 'Surely that's not necessary, Andrew. Anton will accompany Amalia home.'

'I need the air,' he said cuttingly, and Justina put a defensive hand to her throat.

'Then—then I'll come, too,' she stated defiantly.

Andrew frowned. 'You've never ridden with me before.'

'I know. But I need the exercise,' Justina insisted.

Amalia looked bored by the whole affair. 'I'm perfectly capable of riding home alone,' she said coldly.

'We wouldn't think of it,' said Justina firmly, and at least had the satisfaction of knowing she had succeeded in winning this particular round.

Putting only a thick cardigan over her sweater, Justina had Anton saddle her mare for her and swung up on to the animal's back without assistance. Amalia mounted more slowly, allowing Andrew to assist her. Andrew rode his usual stallion; a chestnut, with the will of a devil when it suited him.

The air was clean and fresh and it was good to be out of the *castelo* for a while. But Justina soon grew tired of the cantering pace Amalia maintained and giving the mare her head allowed her to gallop swiftly away from them, down the slope and along the bank of the river. It was beautiful there, in the shade of the pines that grew close to the water's edge and the scents and smells were enchanting. The dappled waters were less turbulent now than they had been the night before when the rain was filling the sheds and sending the water tumbling down to fill the banks. Now only the sucking sound of the water along the river's edge, and the brilliant plumage of the heron as it swooped down to snare its prey disturbed the stillness of the afternoon air.

Glancing round, Justina could see the others following her, and behind them, at a discreet distance, Anton. He accompanied Justina almost everywhere, and it was rather touching to know he was never far away.

Digging in her heels again, she cantered on, telling herself that she didn't care that her behaviour might be interpreted as childish. Riding to her had always been a natural pastime, but the slow, artificial pace Amalia maintained made a mockery of the word. She was merely using the animal as a means of transport, not finding enjoyment in the actual act.

They crossed the river at a shallow point and rode on up the opposite bank to where the trees were brilliant with flame-coloured blossom. Occasionally now they passed small dwellings used by the farm workers, and from time to time a careless child would run into their path.

It was growing later, and the sun was beginning to slide behind the mountains casting long shadows across the lushness of the valley. From above came the cry of a night bird, and the rushing swoop of an eagle from its lofty perch.

Justina brought the mare to a halt and looked back at the others, closer now that she had slowed her pace, and Anton dug in his heels and galloped past them to reach her first. He smiled, and Justina returned his warm greeting.

Andrew and Amalia reached them a few moments later, and Andrew reined in his mount. 'Anton will accompany you from here,' he said, nodding commandingly at the boy. 'And I will escort—my wife—home.'

Amalia glanced at the boy at Justina's side. 'There's no need, you know,' she replied coolly. 'Anton can return with you.' She smiled sardonically. 'I can ensure you I do not require an escort.'

Justina bit her lips. Amalia was being deliberately scathing. Didn't Andrew notice?

However, Andrew made no demur, and with a casual word of goodbye, Amalia cantered away. Looking after her, Justina wondered, rather uncharitably, whether Andrew himself had not been glad of Amalia's refusal to accept Anton's escort. After all, it relieved him of the necessity of riding home alone with her.

With a tightening of her stomach muscles, Justina

tossed the mare's reins, and before either of the men was aware of what she was about to do, she galloped away, leaning low over the mare's head, talking to her softly as she allowed the animal to move swiftly across the turf.

She was at the river giving the horse a drink when Andrew and Anton cantered up to join her, but she was unprepared for Andrew's anger as he swung to the ground and after tying the stallion's reins caught her arm, wrenching her round to face him, his face contorted in the fading light.

'I'm growing a little tired of these exhibitions, Justina!' he bit out harshly. 'Since Amalia's arrival this afternoon there's been one scene after another, and I will not have it! Do you understand me?'

Justina struggled to free herself, but she was helpless against his strength, and Anton looked on unhappily, not knowing what to do.

'You—you're hurting me!' she cried painfully. 'And I don't make scenes! Surely I'm entitled to defend myself when attacked!'

'And when were you attacked?'

'When—when you came to my room, you practically forced your way in—'

'That's right. Had you left the door unlocked in the first place there would have been no need for any unpleasantness.'

'Oh, wouldn't there?' Justina was indignant. 'I'm not a child, Andrew.'

'Then stop behaving like one!'

'How—how dare you?'

'I dare because I am sick and tired of your idiotic behaviour! You say our marriage was not a normal one before the crash—well, surprise, surprise! I believe it!'

Justina's lips parted tremulously. 'You don't understand!' she exclaimed.

'Oh, but I do.' His lips twisted. 'Get on your horse! We're going back to the *castelo*!' And swinging up on to his own stallion he rode away leaving Justina vaguely tearful to confront Anton's anxious solicitude.

When Justina arrived back at the *castelo* she went straight up to see her aunt, and after reassuring herself that the old lady was sleeping peacefully she went to her room. She half expected to find Andrew there. Somehow she sensed she had not heard the last of his anger, but he was not around and the door between their two rooms was closed firmly.

Justina moved about unhappily. Things were going from bad to worse, and she had no way of knowing how to stop them.

Dinner was a silent meal. Juana was present, of course, and Justina was growing increasingly thankful for her appearances. At least it avoided the inevitable difficulties involved in dining alone with the man she had claimed to be her husband.

When the meal was over, Andrew disappeared, and

Justina dared not ask him where he was going. She assumed he had gone to his room and therefore it was a surprise later, when, on her way to bed, she called in on her aunt and found him there, sitting beside the bed reading. Nurse Gomez was nowhere to be seen, and Justina could only assume he was giving her a break as she had once done. But as he made no effort to explain, Justina was forced to go away again, seeking the silence of her own room.

She showered and undressed and slid into bed, certain she would not sleep, but in fact she was exhausted, and she knew nothing after her head touched the pillow.

In the morning, she awoke with the unhappy feeling of something unpleasant hanging over her head. For a few moments she couldn't remember what it was, and then recollections of the previous day came to plague her mind.

Shaking her head, she slid out of bed and after bathing dressed in cream cotton trousers and a red shirt blouse, the long sleeves of which she folded back to her forearms. Brushing her hair, she left it loose and descended the stairs to the hall with some trepidation.

Andrew was already in the small dining room, and she joined him reluctantly. 'Good morning,' she said, taking her seat. 'Have you heard how my aunt is this morning?'

He looked up from a plate of bacon and eggs which

Benita had prepared especially for him and his eyes were guarded. 'Yes. She's improving slowly, just as Ramirez predicted.'

'Oh! Oh, good.' Justina moved the knife beside her plate uncomfortably. 'I—I didn't realise you were sitting with my aunt last evening.'

He finished his breakfast and pushed his plate aside, wiping his mouth with a napkin. 'I didn't know I had to give notice to you of my actions,' he said chillingly.

Justina coloured. 'You—you don't!' She sighed. 'Oh, look, can't we forget all yesterday's unpleasantness and be civil with one another again?'

Benita appeared at that moment with some fresh coffee and when she saw Justina she smiled and asked what she would like.

'Nothing to eat, thank you, Benita,' Justina refused politely. 'Just coffee.'

Benita looked concerned, but she said nothing, and after she had gone, Andrew said sharply: 'There's no point in starving yourself. You already have a strained look about you.'

Justina was indignant. 'Thank you!' she said shortly.

He sighed now. 'Don't be so touchy! If all this elaborate attempt at apology is to be shattered at the first confrontation there's not much point in beginning it, is there?'

Justina poured herself some black coffee and stirred

it slowly. 'No woman likes to be told she looks a mess,' she defended herself.

Andrew uttered a curse under his breath. 'I didn't say you looked a mess. I said you looked strained. And so you do. But it's not unattractive. Dark rings round those big brown eyes give you a faintly haunted air, that's decidedly appealing.'

Justina bent her head. 'Oh! Oh, I see.'

He thrust back his chair and rose abruptly to his feet. 'For goodness' sake,' he muttered, 'don't get the wrong idea. I have no intention of taking up where I left off the other evening! It's that that's caused this tension between us, and I'm sorry. But I am only a man, and that's my only excuse. I'm beginning to realise you were not fooling when you said you had nervous trouble, and I'm sorry.'

Justina stared at him in amazement. The last thing she had expected from him was an apology, and now it had come she found herself wishing it had not. He was right when he said the tension between them stemmed from his behaviour the other evening, but he would have been shocked if he had known exactly what Justina really felt about that affair.

'So you can relax,' he went on grimly. 'And stop acting like a terrified rabbit every time I come near you.'

Justina tried to drink her coffee. She knew the narcotic content would help to calm her, but the liquid stuck in her throat and she almost choked before getting it down.

But before she could say anything more, there was a noise in the courtyard and presently Doctor Ramirez strolled into the room.

'Good morning,' he said, smiling at them both cheerfully. 'I know it is early, but I have a lot of calls to make and I thought I would come and see your aunt first, Justina.'

Justina was glad of his intervention, and she stood down her scarcely touched cup of coffee and indicated the steaming jug.

'Will you have some coffee, doctor?'

To her surprise Ramirez shook his head. 'Thank you, no. I'll see your aunt first, Justina. Will you come with me?'

Justina shrugged. 'Of course, if you want me to.' A faint feeling of foreboding touched her at his words. What was wrong now? Why should he want her to accompany him to examine her aunt? Had he some bad news for her? Or was it something to do with the man at her side?

As they mounted the stairs together Ramirez put his hand into his inside pocket and withdrew an envelope and handed it to her. 'This arrived from the *presidente* this morning,' he said. 'It was delivered to me from the airport at Voltio by helicopter. There was a note asking me to give you the letter when we were alone.'

'From Luis?' Justina stared at the white envelope in her hands, 'I see.'

Ramirez looked at her intently. 'What's wrong, Justina? Why should this letter cause you to look so—so scared?'

Justina looked up. 'I'm not scared, doctor. Th—thank you for delivering it to me. Excuse me.'

'Of course. I will see you later, before I leave.'

'Yes.' Justina nodded and when they reached the landing they parted, she making her way quickly to her own room.

Once there she slit open the envelope with trembling fingers. She knew what she was about to read. Luis's words were brief and to the point:

The authorities in Rio have identified the passengers aboard the aircraft. Is it possible that you could come to Queranova for a few days? There are matters to discuss that cannot be written in a letter.

There was no mention of names, nothing really to identify which passengers and what aircraft he was speaking about. He had protected himself well.

Justina tore the note into shreds and dropped them into her waste basket, then she paced restlessly about the room. She would have to go to Queranova, of course. She could not refuse. Luis had been very patient with her, very understanding; she had no choice but to obey his request.

Going downstairs again, she found Juana in the lounge, sewing as usual. 'Good morning, *senhora*,' she intoned politely. 'Doctor Ramirez is here—with your aunt.'

'Yes, I know.' Justina nodded absently. 'Where—where is my husband?'

'He was here a few moments ago,' observed Juana, applying her needle to the cushion cover she was embroidering. 'I expect he has gone out to the stables.'

'Yes, perhaps so.' Justina bit her lip thoughtfully. 'Tell me, Juana, do you think my aunt would mind if I went to Queranova for a few days?'

Juana laid her sewing aside. 'Queranova, *senhora?*' She was obviously surprised.

'Yes. To see Luis and Morgana.'

Juana shook her head. 'Is this the time for visiting, *senhora?*' She sounded reproachful.

'Doctor Ramirez thinks it's a good idea,' Justina defended herself.

'What do I think is a good idea?' The doctor had entered the room behind her and had heard her final comment.

Justina turned quickly. 'My—my visiting Luis and Morgana for a few days,' she explained.

The doctor raised his eyebrows. 'But when I mentioned this yesterday, you said there was no need—'

'I—I know. But I've had second thoughts.'

'I see.' Doctor Ramirez frowned. 'Luis did not send you bad news, I hope.' He drew out his case of cheroots. 'Morgana is well?'

'I suppose—I mean—yes, of course. He—He's invited me for a visit, that's all. To be company for Morgana, I suppose.' She crossed her fingers behind her back as she spoke. It was true that once one entangled oneself in a web of deceit, one became more entangled trying to get free.

'I see.' Ramirez shrugged. 'Well, naturally I approve. In the circumstances, it will do you good to get away for a while. When do you expect to leave?'

Justina hesitated. 'Perhaps—tomorrow?'

'Excellent. You will use the helicopter to Voltio, of course.'

'Could I?'

'I don't see why not, as it's there. I'll send a message to the airport to expect you. Have you told Andrew?'

'Not yet.'

Ramirez nodded, lighting his cheroot. 'I expect he will enjoy the opportunity to see more of the country—'

'What do you mean?' Justina stared at him.

'Well, he will be going with you, naturally.'

'No! That is—I thought he might prefer to stay here.'

'Nonsense. It will do you both good. Don't you agree, Juana?'

'If you think it is fitting that they should be away at such a time,' murmured Juana unhappily.

Ramirez made an impatient exclamation. 'Do not be such a pessimist, Juana. Renata is not dead yet, and nor is she likely to be in the few days Justina and Andrew will be away. It is only fair that they should have this break.'

Justina moved uncomfortably. This was not at all going as she had planned. She had banked on Ramirez's assistance, but she had not thought he would be so adamant about her husband accompanying her.

'Will you have some coffee now, doctor?' she asked, unable to allow him to leave without offering their hospitality.

'Thank you, that would be very nice.' Ramirez nodded his thanks and with a helpless gesture Justina disappeared to find the cook. When she returned the worst had happened. Andrew was standing before the fireplace, and Ramirez was explaining how Justina had had a letter from her cousin that morning asking her to visit with them for a few days.

'Is this true?' Andrew's jaw tightened as he looked at Justina's taut features.

'Yes, as a matter of fact, it is.' Justina placed the tray she had brought in on a low table. Then she straightened and looked at him squarely. 'But I explained to Doctor Ramirez that you would not want to accompany me, just to visit relatives.'

Andrew's eyes narrowed. 'Why should you say that? Of course I'd like to come.'

Justina heaved a deep breath. 'I thought you would prefer to stay here,' she said abruptly.

'Why?'

Justina turned away, unable to trust herself not to break down in front of him. She wanted to scream with the complexity of it all.

'I told you,' Ramirez was saying. 'It will be a break for both of you. I'll tell Ramon you'll drive up to the air-strip around ten, shall I?'

'Fine.' Andrew took over the acceptance, and Justina poured the coffee and said nothing. It was out of her hands, and she would have to relax soon or her nerves would snap completely.

CHAPTER TEN

THE FOLLOWING morning they drove out to the air-strip in the Landrover. It was a beautiful morning, the sun high in the heavens, the sky an incredibly deep shade of blue. There was mist on the mountain, though, shrouding the ragged slopes in its wraithlike folds, hiding the peaks where so many people had lost their lives.

The pilot of the helicopter was known to Justina. He was a personal friend of Luis's, and she guessed he had been detailed to remain until she reached some sort of a decision. Luis had known she would be unable to refuse his command without good reason.

Her aunt, of course, was unaware of their departure. She was still under sedation, and Ramirez had promised that they would probably see some improvement on their return. Justina had gone cold at his words. Not because she did not welcome her aunt's progress, but simply because she had no way of knowing whether the man she called Andrew would be returning with her. If Luis had some definite news of his identity, it was possible the charade would soon be over. The realisation terrified her. While she told herself she longed to be free of the net of deceit she had tangled herself in, she also knew that the *castelo* would be a cold and empty place without this man.

The flight to Voltio was soon over, and they boarded Luis's private plane to fly to Queranova. The helicopter pilot said goodbye to them, and another pilot took the controls of the small jet.

Throughout the journey, they had spoken little. What conversation there had been had been conducted through the medium of the helicopter pilot and later through the pilot of the jet. If Justina had expected Andrew to ask questions, she was disappointed, and if the luxury of their means of transport impressed him, he certainly did not show it. On the contrary, he showed more interest in the mechanics of the thing, and he and the pilot seemed to find plenty to talk about.

It was at times like this when Justina wondered about him. How was it possible for him to recall in such detail things of this nature? And on those occasions when he had mentioned recollections of his racing days was he really serious, or was he simply making things easier for her? She could never be certain, and soon it wouldn't matter one way or the other.

She wondered what she would tell her aunt if she returned alone. Would she simply say Andrew had had to return to England? Or could she go so far as to tell her that their marriage was breaking up and he would not be coming back? The situation was no nearer a solution now than it had been on her arrival

in Monteraverde, and she stared unseeingly through
the port at her side of the plane, unable to find a
satisfactory thought in her brain.

At least during these weeks at the *castelo* she had
been able to put the memories of her husband's bru-
tality to the back of her mind. She was no longer so
vulnerable in that respect. If only her aunt had not
had her heart attack when she did, Justina would not
have thought twice about telling her of Andrew's
death, and then this situation would never have de-
veloped.

But Sergio Manuelo, her aunt's solicitor, had made
it very plain that from his conversations with her aunt
he had ascertained that the old lady was most adamant
that Justina should be married, that she should have
a man to manage her affairs, and whether these ideas
were old-fashioned or not did not matter. Renata was
still very much in control, and Justina had known she
would not have the strength to oppose her at that time.
Besides, it had not begun to signify until her aunt
voiced this obsession to *see* Andrew, to have him
there at the *castelo*, to talk with him. Justina had
never dreamt that her word might be doubted without
the physical evidence to back her up, and learning of
the man at the mission hospital had seemed like a
miracle. But miracles did not happen, and sooner or
later the illusion must be destroyed.

She looked towards the front of the plane where
Andrew—she still had to call him that—had joined

the pilot at the controls and was presently learning
the meanings of the multiple dials and meters before
them. What kind of a man could he be to accept his
amnesia so complacently? Wasn't he anxious that his
memory might not return? Hadn't he any desire to
know for certain he was who she had said he was?

Justina shook her head helplessly. He was an
enigma.

Then she found herself speculating on whom he
might be. He was intelligent, educated, knowledgeable about general things. He could drive expertly,
ride, discuss music and literature. What manner of
occupation might he have been following that he
could disappear for several weeks without trace, without anyone questioning his disappearance? He could
be anything and anybody.

She pondered the possibility that he might be married. Who might his wife be? Was she beautiful? Her
stomach twisted painfully. She found the idea of him
with some other woman just as unacceptable as seeing
him with Amalia yesterday. She was jealous, there
was no denying it; and she knew then, in that moment, that whatever the outcome of this confrontation,
she had fallen in love with him and she would do
anything in her power to keep him ignorant of his
real identity.

When they landed at Queranova, the presidential
car was waiting for them, and only then did Justina's
companion raise his eyebrows.

'Some service!' he remarked wryly.

'Yes.' Justina glanced at him warily. In a dark lounge suit he looked disturbingly attractive, and she wondered what he would do if she were to stretch out her hand and touch him. She had a strong desire to touch him and she had to force herself to think logically about the real reason why they were here.

She glanced down at her own attire critically. She had chosen a pink suede skirt and jacket suit, worn together with a white lace blouse. The jacket had fringing along the arms and along the bottom, and she wore soft white suede boots. It was as though by making herself look as attractive as possible she could ward off the terrible depression that was seeking to overwhelm her.

The Palacio stood in the main square of the town, hedged about by high walls, a remnant of the days when army invasions were not unknown. These days, however, only a police guard patrolled its precincts and they saluted politely, recognising the car if not its occupants.

Luis himself greeted them as they entered the massive reception hall of the building. The hall was tall and majestic, hung with the portraits of past presidents of Monteraverde, and quite magnificent, and Justina noticed Andrew looking about him with obvious interest.

Luis came forward, shaking Andrew's hand and raising Justina's almost to his lips in a purely gallant gesture. 'How delightful!' he said welcomingly. 'We have been expecting you since we received word from Voltio that you had left in the plane. Come through to our sitting room. Morgana is looking forward to seeing you.'

Morgana Salvador was a beautiful young woman, with very fair hair, several shades lighter than Justina's. She rose from the couch on which she had been resting as they entered the sitting room and came towards them slowly. In a short time now their second child was expected, and she gave a rather embarrassed glance at her swollen stomach.

'Hello, Justina,' she said warmly, kissing her cheek. 'So this is—Andrew!'

Justina glanced at Luis sharply, but he shook his head almost imperceptibly, while Justina's companion shook hands with Luis's wife, his face registering his pleasure in her appearance.

'We haven't met before?' he queried softly, and Morgana glanced apprehensively at her husband.

'Of course. But it is some time ago,' inserted Luis swiftly. 'You remember Andrew, don't you, Morgana?'

'Er—vaguely,' Morgana temporised awkwardly. 'We should have something in common, at least. I'm English, too.' Then she sighed. 'Would anyone mind if I sat down? I—well, I get rather tired standing.'

'Of course not.' Justina shook her head, and Luis moved forward swiftly to assist his wife on to the couch. There was a wealth of warmth and understanding in his gesture and Justina envied them their relationship. She glanced at her companion suddenly and saw a strange expression on his face, too. She wondered what he was thinking. What thoughts filled his mind at these moments?

Luis indicated that they all should be seated and offered drinks. It was almost lunchtime and Justina accepted some sherry while Andrew chose his usual Scotch. The two men talked together quite casually about the weather and the speed with which one could get about these days, while Morgana asked Justina how her aunt was, and expressed anxiety upon learning that the old lady had had another attack.

It was all very pleasant and natural. No one would have suspected from the conversation that there was anything disturbing going on below the surface, and yet Justina could sense it, and she was aware that Luis and his wife could sense it, too.

Lunch was announced soon afterwards, and over the meal they chatted about current affairs. Justina found it easy to evolve interest in Morgana's affairs. Their first child, now a plump toddler, was an ideal, and innocent, topic, and both Luis and Morgana were always willing to talk about their son. Justina looked forward to seeing him later. He was cared for by a young nursemaid, and had his meals in the nursery.

But when the meal was over, and coffee had been served, Justina knew that the moment of decision had come. Morgana remarked that Luis had had communication with Sergio Manuelo concerning her aunt's affairs which he wanted to discuss with Justina, while she suggested that Andrew joined her in the lounge for a chat about England.

Everyone was agreeable, although Justina was aware that Andrew's eyes lingered on her rather doubtfully as she left the room with her cousin. What was he thinking now? She asked herself desperately.

In Luis's study, Luis faced her squarely. 'Well, Justina,' he said solemnly, 'I gather he is no nearer regaining his memory.'

'No.' Justina pressed her lips together. 'But you— you've found out who he is.'

'Yes.' Luis offered her a cigarette and when she refused he lit one himself, considering the heavy brass table lighter thoughtfully for a few moments before putting it back on his desk. 'Has nothing happened— nothing that might give you any hint of who he might be?'

'No.' Justina was impatient now. 'Please, Luis, tell me! Who is he?'

'His name is Dominic Hallam. He's an engineer, employed by a firm of constructional engineers in London. Their managing director, Lester Cunningham, is flying out to see him within the next few days.'

'Oh, God!'

Justina put her hands to her temples, sinking down

into the chair beside the desk. Then she looked up, trying to school herself to be calm. 'But why hasn't his disappearance been noticed before this? Heavens, it's weeks!'

'I gather there was some confusion with the Peruvian government,' Luis said slowly.

'The Peruvian government!' Justina was confused. 'What has the Peruvian government to do with this?'

Luis made a deprecatory gesture. 'I'm explaining very badly. I'm sorry. I should have told you first that he was in Rio, en route for Lima. His assignment is to supervise the construction of a rail link over a section of the Andes, and his office in London naturally assumed he was in Peru. When he did not arrive, and no word was forthcoming, the Peruvian government ministry for whom he was to work contacted the London office, but through confusion there, distance being of the essence, I suppose, it wasn't immediately realised that Hallam had not in fact arrived.'

'I see.' Justina looked pale. 'And you say the managing director of this company—'

'Cunningham International,' inserted Luis quickly.

'—yes, this company managing director is flying out here.'

'That's right. I had word from the airline authorities only yesterday.'

Justina shook her head. 'So it's all over.'

Luis sighed, stubbing out his half-smoked cigarette impatiently. 'You knew it would be, sooner or later.

I only hope we can persuade this man that it really was a genuine mistake.'

Justina got to her feet. She felt physically sick. 'What—what else did they tell you about him? I mean—is he married, or anything?'

'That I can not say. The information I have is purely of an impersonal nature.'

Justina heaved a sigh. 'What are we going to do?'

Luis bent his head. 'I don't know.' He walked round the desk. 'Tell me something, Justina: do you know anything about your aunt's finances?'

Justina looked startled. 'Finances?' she echoed. 'What has that to do with this?'

Luis looked slightly discomfited. 'It might have a lot,' he said slowly.

'Why?' Justina stared at him in surprise. 'Why should I know anything about Tia Renata's affairs? And why are you asking me?'

Luis sighed now. 'When I sent you that note yesterday asking you to come here it was more than just anxiety about this man—this Dominic Hallam.'

Justina shook her head. 'Stop talking in riddles, Luis.' Then she halted uncertainly. 'Wait a minute! Morgana said something about Sergio Manuelo contacting you. I—I thought she was just being tactful.'

'No, Manuelo has contacted me. He—well, he has received a communication from your aunt—'

'From Tia Renata?' Justina was astounded. 'But— but she hasn't been well enough to write letters.'

'No, I know. Someone wrote it for her.'

'Who? Nurse Gomez?'

'Knowing your aunt as I do, I hardly think she would entrust a letter of that nature to a stranger.'

'A letter of *what* nature?'

'A letter concerning your aunt's finances!'

Justina was totally confused. 'My aunt's finances?' she echoed. 'Then who did write it? And what did it say?'

'The man your aunt thought was Andrew—Hallam wrote the letter.' Luis stroked his dark sideburns. 'Now do you see how the two things intermingle?'

'Oh, please!' Justina was trembling now. 'What is this all about? Why would she have Andrew write a letter for her? Why not me?' But as she asked herself the question, she recalled the night she had found him in her aunt's room. That night Renata had been too ill, of course, but there had been other nights when she had imagined him in his room. Oh, what had he been saying to her aunt? Or she to him?

'The letter concerned you,' Luis went on. 'As you are aware, your aunt was left a considerable personal fortune on her parents' death, which fortune was expected to be passed on to you.'

'Yes.' Justina nodded.

'Well, your aunt became bored with her lonely existence during the years you were in school, and she contrived an idea of making her money work for her.'

'You mean—on the stock market?'

'That sort of thing. In any event, she consulted no one, not least her solicitor in Queranova, employing another lawyer to handle the business side of her ventures for her.'

'Go on!' Justina could feel the shiver of apprehension cooling her spine.

Luis sighed again. 'Surely what I am about to say becomes obvious. Her original will remained with Manuelo's firm, and so far as anyone here was concerned, she was a wealthy woman. Certainly, she spared no expense to provide you with what she thought was a suitable husband.'

Justina sank down into her chair again. 'She thought Andrew was wealthy,' she breathed unsteadily.

'Of course. As he thought you were. Both your aunt and your late husband were caught by the same hook.' He shrugged, looking down on Justina compassionately.

'So that's why she wanted Andrew here—in Monteraverde! She wanted to be certain I would not be left destitute. She was afraid if I broke with Andrew, she would not have the heart to tell me the truth.'

'I suppose so.' Luis shook his head. 'In any event, once Andrew, or the man she thought was Andrew, appeared, she took the opportunity to have him contact Manuelo and explain the circumstances. Manuelo was horrified, naturally. He blames himself for not taking a closer interest in her affairs.'

Justina shook her head now. 'It's not his fault.'
Then she looked up. 'But—but this means that—that
this man Hallam knows my financial position.'

'I'm afraid so. Although I doubt it matters, in the
circumstances.'

Justina bit her lips hard. 'On the contrary, it matters
a great deal! Can't you see what he's going to think
when he knows the truth? He'll never believe what
we want him to believe! He'll think I grabbed him to
protect myself when all this came out!'

'Why should he think that?'

'Because he will!' exclaimed Justina unhappily.
'Can't you see? He'll think we planned never to tell
him the truth!'

'Oh, Justina! You're dramatising the situation! In
Hallam's position, I'd be so damn glad I knew who
I was again, I wouldn't waste time on recriminations!'

'But you don't know him, Luis! I do!' Justina got
to her feet again, moving restlessly about the room,
pressing her balled fist to her lips.

Luis watched her for a few moments, and then he
said: 'It seems to me that the authorities discovering
his identity at this moment is the best thing that could
have happened.'

'Why do you say that?'

'Because now you know where you stand. On your
own two feet.'

Justina moved her shoulders helplessly. 'Does this
mean the *castelo* will have to be sold?'

'Not necessarily, although the upkeep of a building like that is naturally higher than a smaller house.'

'I see.' Justina made a hopeless gesture. 'So it's all been for nothing. I should have told Manuelo the truth—at the airport.'

'And shocked your aunt? At a time when she was very ill?'

Justina nodded slowly. 'No! No, I couldn't have done that, could I?' She shrugged. 'I should have had to bluff my way out some other way.'

'What do you intend to do now? Are you going to tell him? Do you want me to? Or will you wait until this man Cunningham arrives?'

Justina frowned. 'I suppose I must tell him.'

'Very well. When?'

'Oh, don't rush me, Luis. Give me time to take it in. Right now I'm having difficulty even thinking straight.'

'Of course. I'm sorry.' Luis patted her shoulder. 'Take it easy. Would you like a drink? I have some Scotch here.'

'No, nothing, thanks.' Justina heaved a deep breath. 'I never dreamt anything like this when I got your message. Just imagine—in the space of twenty minutes I've been deprived of a husband and a fortune!'

'Don't be bitter, Justina.'

'I'm not bitter.' Justina managed a faint smile. 'Quite honestly, I feel better about Tia Renata now.

At least I wasn't the only one practising deception. I just wish—I just wish—'

'That this man Hallam had not been available?' Luis queried softly.

Justina bent her head, colour surging into her cheeks. 'Perhaps.'

Luis uttered a sudden exclamation. 'For God's sake, Justina! You can't mean that you've become involved with this man? You haven't—you haven't—'

'Slept with him, Luis?' she challenged, her eyes bright with unshed tears. 'Oh, no, I haven't done that. Perhaps I should have done.'

Luis was aghast. 'You can't be serious!'

'Oh, but I am.'

'You mean—you've allowed yourself to become attracted to him?' Luis smote his fist into the palm of his hand. 'God, Justina, why?'

She shrugged. 'Does one choose? Who knows,' she went on bitterly, 'if I had allowed him the rights of a normal husband, I might have been as secure as Morgana by now, and then what could he have done?'

'Morgana?' Luis chewed at his lip. 'Pregnant, you mean.'

'Of course.' Justina tugged at a strand of dull gold hair. 'Does that shock you?'

Luis sighed. 'Of course it shocks me. After what you told me about Andrew—about your attitude to-wards—towards men...'

Justina pressed her palms together, resting the tips

of her fingers against her lips, prayer-like. 'I know. Crazy, isn't it? But I'm not like that with—with him with Dominic.' She said the word slowly, savouring it. It was such a nicer name than Andrew anyway.

Luis put a hand to his forehead. 'I thought you just said that you—that you and he—'

'We didn't go to bed together, no.' Justina raised her dark eyebrows. 'But we have...well...kissed.'

'Good heavens!' Luis was obviously out of his depth. 'Justina, it seems to me you've been taking the most ridiculous risks—'

'Yes, I have, haven't I?' Justina's lips drooped. 'Oh, why did this man Cunningham have to come here now? Why couldn't—Dominic have just disappeared?'

Luis walked heavily towards the door. 'Don't be silly, Justina. You're not a child. You know things like that don't happen.'

Justina followed him towards the door. 'Thank you, anyway, Luis,' she murmured. 'For everything!'

He turned, reaching out to take the handle. 'Don't thank me, Justina,' he advised, rather grimly. 'It's not over yet.'

CHAPTER ELEVEN

THERE WAS an official banquet at the Palacio that evening to which, of course, Dominic and Justina were not invited. Instead, they spent the evening in the private rooms of the Palacio with Morgana. It was a very pleasant evening, but Dominic was relieved when it was over and he could go to his room. For the moment he had sufficient to occupy his mind, and he knew, now that he was here in the capital, he should make some effort to identify himself and relieve the feelings of his friends and associates back home.

But this situation, which had begun almost lightheartedly, was becoming more complex every day, and the events of the past few days had served to show him exactly how irresponsibility could lead to disaster.

When he first assumed the identity of this unknown Andrew Douglas, he had been curious to know why Justina should have required to make such a claim, but after living at the *castelo* for some time he had begun to appreciate her position and the strength of will power of her aunt, Renata de la Roca. Why Renata should have been so concerned that Justina was content had not become clear until she had asked him to write that letter to Sergio Manuelo.

194

The old lady was practically penniless, and she was relying on Justina's husband to support her after she was dead. She had even told him of her earlier anxieties, and of how she had considered suggesting to Father Juan that Justina should enter the convent.

Dominic had listened, at first with indifference, and then with dismay, his emotions developing along with his relationship with Justina. His initial reaction to her deception had been one of contempt; he had felt no mercy for her or cared what the ultimate outcome of this masquerade might be. But later, so many things had helped to change his attitude.

Unknowingly, by her attitude towards him, and by certain things Renata had told him, Dominic had built up a composite picture of Justina's husband, and the composition was not pleasing. No one could deny that Justina's immediate reaction to any attempt at tenderness had produced a real feeling of terror, and when he had touched her she had flinched away from him instantly.

Again, he had foolishly imagined that perhaps she was made that way, that perhaps she was one of those women incapable of responding to a man's advances. He had even been prepared to believe that there had been some break-up in their marriage caused by her frigidity.

But then the night they had gone to Amalia Garcia's house he had put the theory to the test, and discovered that not only was she a flesh and blood woman, warm and responsive, but that he responded to her in a way he had determined he would never respond again.

And that was when the real agony had begun. Because in spite of everything that had gone before, in spite of the deception, he had begun to want her, really want her, not as a fleeting interlude, speedily concluded with no strings on either side, but for keeps, to share his life with him, to be the mother of the children he had never thought to have. He *loved* her, and she was another man's wife!

Then, before he had had chance to consider the difficulties involved, there had come this trip to Queranova, and the insistent knowledge that this was to be the end of their association, that this cousin of hers, Luis Salvador, had somehow discovered his real identity and perhaps the authorities were demanding his return.

But nothing had been said yet, even though Justina had been observing him surreptitiously all evening, and Dominic was aware that he was as guilty as she by maintaining his silence. Not only that, his friend and employer Lester Cunningham, deserved to be informed of the real facts of the case. He had taken up quite enough of their time in this crazy charade, and now it was only right that he should identify himself and take up his real life again.

Flinging off his jacket, he began to unbutton his shirt, walking to the windows and looking out on the lights of the city below. It all looked so calm and peaceful, vastly different from the turmoil of his thoughts.

Under the shower, he tried to assimilate his position. It would be a simple matter for him to contact the British Ambassador, identify himself, explain the circumstances, with the backing of Doctor Ramirez, and be flown back to London immediately.

But what about Justina? What would she do? Where was the real Andrew Douglas? Did he intend to join her here? It didn't seem likely when she had taken the risk of identifying *him* as her husband. Surely she would not have done that if there had been any chance of Andrew suddenly turning up. So where was he? In England?

Dominic shook his head. Just thinking of another man with Justina made something inside his stomach crawl, and he put out a hand and grabbed a huge bathsheet, wrapping it about his lean body grimly. What a hell of a situation!

Dried, he put on a silk dressing gown and flung himself on his bed, lighting a cigar automatically. His eyes flickered round the room as he inhaled deeply. It was a beautiful room, he had to admit it, pale mahogany furniture blending well with a chocolate brown carpet and apricot covers and curtains, an adjoining door in the wall between his room and Justina's.

His lips twisted. Obviously the Salvadors knew he

was not who Justina said he was. Surely even in this out-of-the-way country men and women did not have separate rooms as a normal situation. No, it was obvious that here, as in the *castelo*, every effort had been made to keep their relationship on a wholly platonic basis.

He stared at the lighted tip of his cigar. Maybe he had been a fool, he thought savagely. Maybe he was wrong about Justina. Maybe he should have demanded his rights straight off, instead of waiting, respecting her fears.

Then he sighed. He couldn't have done that. He was not an animal. He was a human being. And he had never found it necessary to force his attentions on any woman. On the contrary, they had usually been more than willing to comply. Women like Amalia Garcia, for example.

He tapped ash into the heavy tray on the table beside his bed. Amalia Garcia! He shook his head. He had deliberately sought her company the morning after his confrontation with Justina in an effort to prove to himself that he was making a fool of himself over the woman who had claimed him as her husband, but it had been no good. The moment he had arrived back at the *castelo* and found Justina's door locked against him, he had wanted to do actual physical violence. And then when she had opened the door and looked at him he had wanted to throw her on the bed and make love to her until she was incapable of denying him ever again. And she would have let him, that was the thing that bugged him most. In his arms she became soft and submissive, and the will to escape was overwhelmed by their physical response to one another. But that wasn't enough, not when her real husband was still in the background, and Dominic refused to be used in that way.

He stubbed out his cigar bitterly, sliding off the bed to pace about the room like a caged lion. It was no good. He couldn't go on like this. One way or other the situation had to be resolved, but God alone knew how that was to be achieved...

The following morning Justina was awake and dressed early. She felt very much like the man who has only a few hours left before the firing squad is due to arrive to kill him, and she was guiltily relieved to learn that Morgana was not feeling well enough to get up that morning and therefore would not be present to observe her distress.

She breakfasted alone in the enormous dining room of the Palacio. Luis always had his meal very early before becoming closeted with his private secretary for the rest of the morning, and when the man she now knew was Dominic Hallam did not appear either Justina felt terribly isolated. Once he learned of his real identity, he would be gone for good, and she might as well make the best of it.

Refusing anything but coffee, she sat a long while

at the damask-covered table with its elaborate accom-
paniments of side tables on which were silver salvers
of every kind of breakfast dish imaginable, wondering
however she was to find the words to say what must
be said. Luis had told her that this man, Lester Cunningham, was due to arrive in a few days. That could
be today, and she was no nearer confessing the truth.
It was frightening. What would he do? What would
he say? There were laws against confining someone
against their will, and no one, knowing Andrew
Douglas's appearance, could imagine that she could
have made the kind of mistake that would have placed
a seal of credulity upon the proceedings. What if he
decided she had taken advantage of his circumstances? What if he decided to prosecute? What de-
fence could she offer? And what might the penalty
be?

She left the table in some distress, half wishing he
would appear at that moment and allow her to purge
herself on the spot.

But after making her way back up to their suite of
rooms and then down again without encountering
him, she rang the bell for the servant and asked if he
knew where her husband might be.

'Why yes, *senhora*,' the tall footman inclined his
head politely. 'Senhor Douglas requested a car quite
early this morning and left soon after eight.'

'He left!' echoed Justina disbelievingly. 'Did—did
he say where he was going?'

'Not exactly, *senhora*. He said something about—about seeing a little of the city, I believe.'

Justina swept her hair behind her ears nervously. 'I see.' She frowned. 'Does—does the *presidente* know of this?'

'I do not think so, *senhora*. Should he have done?'

Justina shook her head impatiently. 'Oh, no, no, I suppose not. Thank you.'

'Yes, *senhora*.'

The footman withdrew and Justina paced about the sitting room where they had been greeted on their arrival the day before. She wondered where he had gone and why. Couldn't he have told her if he was just going sight-seeing? And if he wasn't—where was he?

A cold sweat filmed her brow. Had his memory been brought back by their altered circumstances? Had his conversation with the pilot yesterday sparked off a chain of remembrance?

Oh, if only Luis was not so busy! If only she could see him—talk to him.

But she dared not interrupt while her cousin was engrossed with matters of state, so she spent her time flicking uninterestedly through magazines and going backwards and forwards to the entrance hall every time she heard the sound of a car in the courtyard.

But lunchtime arrived and Dominic had still not returned and when Luis left his study, Justina was waiting for him, her face pale and anxious.

He looked at her questioningly, and then dismissing his staff he exclaimed: 'Justina, what is it? What has happened?' He took her arm and led her back into his study. 'Come now. What is wrong?'

Justina trembled violently. 'He's disappeared!' she stated unevenly.

'Disappeared?' Luis frowned. 'What do you mean—disappeared?'

'Dominic. He's gone. He asked for a car this morning, and he left soon after eight o'clock.'

'What!' Luis was flabbergasted now. 'But who gave permission for him to use one of the official cars?'

'Did he need permission?' Justina grimaced. 'Oh, well, I suppose Morgana said as much last evening. She said if we wanted to go out just to ask for a car.'

'I see.' Luis nodded. 'And he has gone, without telling you where.'

'Yes.' Justina heaved a sigh. 'Oh, Luis, what am I going to do?'

'Calm yourself.' Luis chewed hard at his lower lip, and at that moment there was a knock at the study door.

Justina started violently, and Luis called: 'Come!' rather impatiently.

One of the Palacio secretaries stood on the threshold. 'There is a message for you, Excellency,' he stated politely, holding out the note in his hand.

Luis nodded. 'Very well, give it to me. You may go.'

After the man had closed the door again Luis opened the note and Justina moved about unhappily, hoping that whatever message it was it wouldn't take Luis away for the rest of the day. But Luis's sudden exclamation brought a shaft of fear to her consciousness, and her attention was riveted on his face.

'This message is from the British Embassy,' Luis said quietly. 'Informing me that a Senhor Lester Cunningham arrived there earlier this morning.'

Justina swallowed with difficulty. 'Lester Cunningham!'

'Yes. This man Hallam's employer whom I told you was flying out to see him.'

Justina shook her head. 'Does—does the note mention—Dominic?'

'No. It is merely an informatory note concerning this man Cunningham. I asked to be informed of his arrival.'

'Then where is Dominic?'

'I don't know.' Luis sighed. 'Justina, are you sure this man Hallam has no idea of his real identity?'

Justina frowned. 'Of—course. Why do you ask?

Luis shook his head now. 'I don't know. I just find the whole affair somewhat disturbing.'

'What are we going to do?'

'What can we do?' Luis was impatient. 'Justina,

this situation is of your own making. We must just sit and wait.'

'And the official car? Don't you care that it's missing, too?'

'My dear Justina, if you think I am about to institute a search for a missing vehicle in the hope of tracing this man Hallam in the process, you are very much mistaken.'

Justina bent her head. 'I see.'

Luis gave her an exasperated look. 'I will ring the garage, and ask them to inform me when the car returns,' he said heavily. 'And that is all.'

'Yes, Luis.' Justina was subdued.

Sighing, Luis lifted the intercom and dialled the Palacio garages. When the mechanic answered, he explained what he wanted, and then he gave another ejaculation.

'When?' he snapped. 'And where did the chauffeur leave this man?'

There was silence for a moment and Justina looked at Luis with agonised eyes so that he put his hand over the mouthpiece, cutting off the sound of their conversation, and said bleakly: 'The car was returned to the garages over an hour ago. The mechanic is presently contacting the driver to find out where he left Hallam.'

'Oh, God!' Justina pressed the palms of her hands to her mouth.

A few moments later Luis nodded, and said:

'Thank you,' in a curiously taut voice and rang off. Then he said heavily: 'I somehow do not think you are going to have to make any confessions, Justina. The driver dropped Hallam at the British Embassy!'

It was late in the afternoon before Justina decided what she must do. There had been no further word from either the British Embassy or from Dominic himself, and she knew by now the worst must have happened, the worst being that he had learned the truth.

She felt an immense feeling of weariness and she no longer had the strength left with which to fight it. All she wanted was the chance to escape to somewhere remote and quiet, where she could lick her mental wounds in peace.

The *castelo*!

She sought Luis about four-thirty and told him what she wanted to do. At first he demurred, but when he realised she really was at the very end of her endurance, he gave in, realising that it had all been too much for her. He could deal with anything that came up, and at least he was not emotionally involved. He knew the agonies of mental torture; he had suffered some of them himself in the past before he knew for certain that Morgana loved him.

So he arranged for her to leave in the presidential plane, making her excuses to Morgana, and avoiding the inevitable ethics of the situation.

It was late at night when Justina arrived back at the *castelo*, tired but unutterably relieved to be back where she belonged. There would be questions, no doubt, Juana would see to that, and her aunt would want to know where Andrew was when she recovered, but right now, nothing mattered except that she should go to bed and sleep and sleep and sleep... Justina's aunt died a few days later without ever properly recovering consciousness. And Justina realised from Antonio Ramirez's face that he had never expected her to recover at all. In fact he had probably imagined Renata would die while Justina and her husband were away in Queranova.

Justina's explanations that Andrew had had to return to England unexpectedly had met with no reaction, and after the funeral she saw no reason to explain to Juana the real circumstances. After all in a few days, after her aunt's affairs were cleared up, Juana would have to be dismissed and the *castelo* would most probably be sold. She did not tell Juana this. It would be time enough for that once the state of her late aunt's affairs was made known, and there was no need to worry the elderly companion at a time when she was already upset over Renata's demise.

But before Renata's estate was settled, Justina received another letter, surprisingly from Andrew's solicitors in London. She had thought Andrew's estate settled, but apparently there were still some matters to be cleared up and she had been contacted with a view to her coming to London to deal with them.

The letter threw Justina into a turmoil. The very last place she had ever expected to visit again was England, and the thought of travelling all that way just to deal with Andrew's affairs did not appeal to her, particularly not now. She wanted nothing to remind her of him.

So she wrote back explaining that her aunt had recently died, and that she did not feel up to travelling all that way at this time and could the papers be sent out to her.

But the second letter from the solicitors stated in no uncertain terms that her presence in England was absolutely essential, and that she should make arrangements to travel immediately.

Justina was at a loss. There was no one to discuss her anxieties with. She dared not contact Luis again, after that other fiasco, and as she had had no word from him either she supposed nothing further had happened. She lived in fear of receiving some kind of summons demanding that she go to court and explain her reasons for the deception to some unforgiving magistrate.

But nothing had happened, and now she was being asked to leave the country for vastly different reasons.

Eventually she decided she would have to go. She explained to Juana that she was going to England, and Juana naturally assumed that her husband had sent for her. Justina did not disillusion her. It was simpler that way. She despised herself for it, but she seemed to be becoming an adept at taking the easy way out.

She landed in London on a cold afternoon in late March, when eddies of rain drizzled down the cab windows, and a chill wind reminded one that winter was still making its presence felt.

She booked in at a small hotel near Hyde Park, and spent the rest of the day in her room. She would contact the solicitors in the morning, but the journey had exhausted her and there were lines of fatigue round her eyes.

In the morning, nothing looked much better. The rain had eased, but it was still cold, and not even the watery sun peeping through the clouds could lift her mood of depression.

After breakfasting in the hotel dining room, Justina put a call through to the offices of Messrs Bennett, Allwyn and Forster, explaining that she had arrived in London the previous day and was able to meet them at whatever time they found suitable.

The young solicitor who dealt with her call arranged, after some delay, that she should visit the offices that afternoon, and Justina thanked him politely and rang off. She couldn't imagine what difficulties they had run into that should have brought her back here to London, but she was too tired and mentally exhausted to make much demur now that the journey was over.

She spent the morning in the hotel, much to the management's surprise. They had obviously put her down as a tourist and the fact that she was not visiting any of the tourist haunts seemed to them rather unusual. However, Justina ignored the speculative glances directed to her corner of the lounge and took an early lunch before setting out for Lincoln's Inn.

The offices of Messrs Bennett, Allwyn and Forster were unimpressive, a grey stone-faced building that stretched upwards for several floors. She had been here before and the receptionist smiled in recognition.

'Mrs Douglas, isn't it?' she questioned, as Justina approached her desk.

'That's right,' Justina nodded, glancing down automatically at the blue wool trouser suit she was wearing to ascertain the neatness of her appearance. She had secured her hair in a french pleat to avoid a windswept look, and she felt confident the mature style suited her. Certainly she felt years older than the last time she had visited the building.

The receptionist used her intercom and then looked up. 'Up the stairs, the first door to your right, Mrs Douglas,' she directed with a smile.

'Thank you.'

Justina ascended the flight of narrow stairs slowly, and reaching the landing saw several doors. But the receptionist had said the first door to the right, so she knocked firmly on the panels.

'Come in!' called a masculine voice, and turning

the handle she opened the door and entered a wide, well-lit room, with a russet carpet and a large oak desk.

These things she registered automatically, but her eyes went straight to the man who was standing in front of the desk leaning casually against its heavy width, his arms folded across his broad chest. Dressed in a grey lounge suit and immaculate linen, his hair smooth and dark, he was the epitome of a London businessman, but he was more than that to Justina, and she stared at him in astonishment, tempted to back out of the door once more, convinced she was suffering delusions.

Shaking her head slowly, she murmured almost under her breath: 'I—I'm sorry. I must have got the wrong room.'

Dominic Hallam straightened and moved forward abruptly taking the handle of the door from her unresisting fingers and closing the door firmly. Then he walked past her again to the desk, and turning said: 'You haven't got the wrong room, Justina. I sent for you.'

Justina just stared at him. 'You sent for me,' she echoed blankly.

'That's right,' Dominic nodded, helping himself to a cigar from the box on the desk. 'Won't you sit down?'

Justina shook her head again. 'No—no, thank you.'

She glanced round apprehensively. 'Why—why should you do such a thing?'

Dominic lit his cigar before replying, then he shrugged. 'Perhaps I wanted to bring you back into this country so that I could have you arrested for confining a stranger in your home and pretending he was your husband?' he remarked cruelly.

Justina flinched. 'You—would do that?'

Dominic looked at her for a long moment and then he shook his head abruptly. 'No! No, I wouldn't do that.'

Justina swallowed hard. 'Has—has your memory returned?'

Dominic's lips twisted. 'What if I told you my memory returned before you removed me from the clinic?'

Justina gasped. 'That wouldn't—that couldn't be true!'

'Why not?'

'Well, why would you permit me to do such a thing if you already knew who you were?'

'Maybe I was curious.'

Justina sank down weakly into the chair now, no longer trusting her legs to support her. 'You're confusing me,' she murmured huskily.

'No more than you've confused me, believe me,' observed Dominic bleakly.

'And—and you knew who you were—all along?'

'That's right.'

'But why did you do it?'

'Why did you?'

Justina shook her head. 'For purely selfish reasons, I suppose,' she said bitterly. 'I didn't want to tell my aunt that—that Andrew was dead.'

'No, I know that now.' Dominic regarded her intently.

'You know?' Justina looked up at him helplessly.

'Yes, I know. Luis told me.'

'Luis? You've spoken to Luis?'

'Oh, yes. For a long time I spoke with Luis.' Dominic chewed his lower lip hard. 'For God's sake, Justina, why did you run away?' These last words were spoken in a different tone, almost as though they were torn from him against his will.

Justina lowered her lids, hiding her eyes from the intentness of his. 'Surely that's obvious,' she said unevenly. 'I knew—after word came that that man Cunningham had arrived—that you would soon know the truth, and I was too cowardly to face you!'

He muttered an expletive, grinding out his cigar in the ash tray. 'But why? Why couldn't you have waited? You knew I would come back.'

'How did I know that? How could I be sure what you would do? You sent no word. You just disappeared!'

'I know, but try and understand it from my point of view. I went to the Embassy that morning to explain the situation to the Ambassador, not realising that Lester had already arrived. Hell, the Ambassador in Queranova happens to have gone to school with him, and naturally as soon as he saw me, the whole thing exploded. God, it took hours to explain. There was so much to tell, and—well, one thing led to another, and before I knew where I was it was pretty late. I guess it was thoughtless, but then Lester thought I'd been pretty thoughtless so far as he was concerned, too, so there you are.'

Justina put a hand to her temples. 'And—and when you saw Luis, what did you tell him?'

'It was more a case of what he told me,' remarked Dominic grimly. 'To begin with, you were missing, and that didn't make for good relations.'

'What do you mean?'

'Hell, what do you think I mean? I could have wrung his bloody neck when he told me he'd allowed you to go hareing back up to the *castelo*. I'd promised Lester I'd return to London with him the following day and I didn't have time then to go chasing after you. Besides, I didn't know then that Andrew Douglas was dead.'

'I—I see.' Justina flushed. 'And now you do.'

'Oh, yes, I know a lot of things. I know how you were manoeuvred into this marriage by your aunt; how the alternative could have been the convent; how Andrew treated you—oh, yes—' as Justina's face burned with hot colour 'oh, yes, I know about that, too. And believe me, in that respect I agree with your cousin. I just wish, in some ways, he was still around for me to teach a lesson to.' Then he raked a hand through his hair. 'God, what a thing to feel! I used not to be so bitter.' He shook his head. 'Anyway, that's beside the point, what else did I learn from friend Luis? Oh, yes, I heard how Douglas and your aunt both thought they were getting the better of one another with this marriage with you as the go-between, and how when you arrived back there after Renata's seizure, you couldn't tell her the truth for obvious reasons. Oh, yes, I think I know pretty well everything about that.'

Justina rose abruptly to her feet. 'Well, I'm glad you're satisfied. And I suppose I should be feeling grateful that you're not about to bring charges, but I just wish you could have put all this down on paper, instead of bringing me all this way—' Her voice broke ignominiously, and she turned away, unable to meet his intent gaze.

Dominic uttered a muffled exclamation, and in a moment he was behind her, his hands hard on her shoulders, dragging her trembling body back against the strength of his.

'What the hell are you talking about, Justina,' he groaned achingly. 'I didn't just bring you here to talk!'

And his mouth sought the soft nape of her neck, with urgent pressure, his fingers threading the pins

from her hair so that it fell about her shoulders like
a heavy silken curtain.

Justina submitted to his touch only a moment, and
then she dragged herself out of his arms, putting the
width of the desk between them. 'No!' she said,
breathlessly. 'No. It—it won't do.'

Dominic's face was dark with anger. 'Why?' he
demanded fiercely. 'Damn you, I know you too well,
Justina. You can't deny you want me to make love
to you!'

Justina smoothed her tumbled hair. 'No, no, I can't
deny that,' she admitted huskily. 'And—and if we'd
stayed in the valley, I know—I know the inevitable
would have happened. And—and I'd have welcomed
that.' He stepped forward, but she held out a hand to
ward him off. 'But it's different now,' she went on
quickly. 'I—you know—at least, I know you know
you're not my husband now, and—and I'm not the
kind of woman you—you might think I am.'

'What in hell do you mean by that?' He sounded
furious.

'I mean—just because I was—well, shameless,
there, I couldn't—I couldn't agree to—to an affair—'

'For God's sake, woman! Am I asking you to have
an affair with me?' he demanded thickly. He strode
across the room, and disregarding her puny efforts to
prevent him, he brought her close against him, pressing her body into his. 'I want to marry you, you crazy
little idiot,' he muttered, burying his face in the thick-

ness of her hair. 'God, if I don't have you soon, I'll go out of my mind!'

Justina brought her head back to look up at him. 'But—but once you said you remembered rows—rows with a wife!' she whispered faintly. 'Was—was that all made up?'

His eyes darkened. 'No. I was married, and we were divorced. But the woman I was married to died afterwards. I have no wife. And nor did I ever intend having another. Until I met you, and your stupid, bloody schemes...' and his mouth met hers, parting her lips with devastating hunger.

It was some time later when Justina forced herself to think coherently again. 'But why did you make me come here? Why didn't you come to the valley?'

Dominic smoothed her hair behind her ears, cupping her face in his hands. 'For several reasons. First of all because I'd promised Lester to give him some of my time.' He half smiled. 'He's been very understanding, doubly so when you consider that I shall soon be taking more time off for a honeymoon. And also because I wanted to see you here, away from the subtle influence of your aunt. I'm sorry she's dead. I should have said that sooner. But right now, there are so many things to be said. And finally, I wanted you here, where you could see where I work, the apartment I live in; my world, in fact. The world you're going to have to inhabit if you become my wife. Do you think you can stand it?'

Justina made a helpless gesture. 'I feel I could live anywhere with you,' she whispered huskily. 'But—but what about the *castelo*? I—I'll have to sell it.'

'Why? Surely its upkeep is not so great. Besides, if you want, and if your country's *presidente* will allow it, it could be our home. My work takes me to the four corners of the world. England is just a base. It's never been really home to me.'

Justina's lips parted. 'Oh, that would be marvellous!' she breathed. 'I don't know how to thank you.'

'You do, you know,' he remarked succinctly, causing the warm colour to flood her cheeks once more.

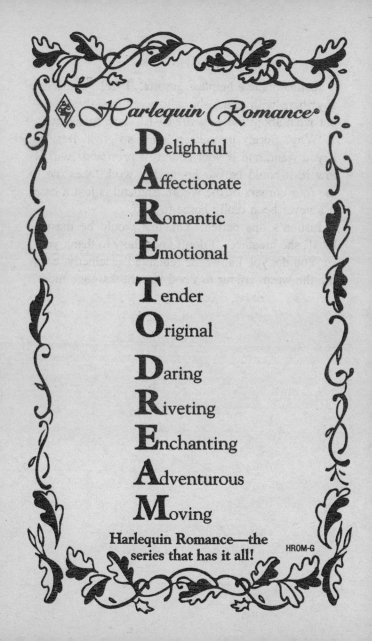

Harlequin Romance®

Delightful

Affectionate

Romantic

Emotional

Tender

Original

Daring

Riveting

Enchanting

Adventurous

Moving

Harlequin Romance—the
series that has it all!

HROM-G

HARLEQUIN Presents

The world's bestselling romance series...
The series that brings you your favorite authors,
month after month:

Helen Bianchin...Emma Darcy
Lynne Graham...Penny Jordan
Miranda Lee...Sandra Marton
Anne Mather...Carole Mortimer
Susan Napier...Michelle Reid

and many more uniquely talented authors!

Wealthy, powerful, gorgeous men...
Women who have feelings just like your own...
The stories you love, set in exotic, glamorous locations...

HARLEQUIN PRESENTS,
Seduction and passion guaranteed!

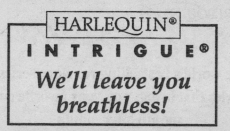

Harlequin®
Historical

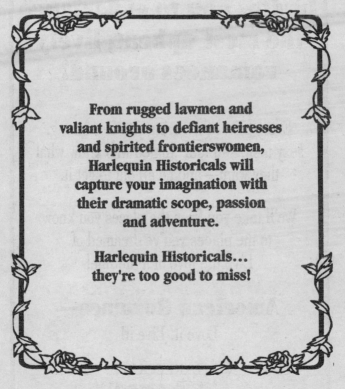

From rugged lawmen and
valiant knights to defiant heiresses
and spirited frontierswomen,
Harlequin Historicals will
capture your imagination with
their dramatic scope, passion
and adventure.

Harlequin Historicals...
they're too good to miss!

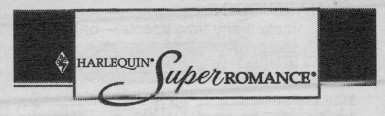

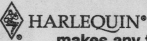